Operator: Harrowers Beyond the Blue Sky

Vol. 2

Aurelet

Cover art by Aurelet

Facebook.com/Aurelet   X.com/@Aurelet212

ISBNs: 979-8-218-46230-7 [ebook]

979-8-218-46231-4 [paperback]

Printed by Kindle Direct Publishing

Prologue

Force-on-Force

The pitter-patter of a late spring rain covered the noise of the operator's footfalls as they made their way around dense brush. The tree canopy above them caught enough of the water droplets to allow them to see clearly. The seven soldiers zigzagged from one tree to the next. Ryder held a closed fist, leading the others trailing to quickly get into cover. Peering through a thermal scope, Ryder swept the area ahead of him, seeing no indication the enemy had been here. Not that the rain made it easy, leaving cold blue curtains where the tree cover was thin.

"Ryder, the enemy hasn't detected you yet. Continue heading west until you reach Michael's Rock."

"Copy that, Commander. Things are going pretty smoothly this time around."

"I'm feeling good about this one. Looks like the captains are going to owe us big time." Misha loudly whispered.

"Cut the chatter, we still got a task to complete." Commander Kurepina cut in. It sounded like she was all in on this plan to Ryder. He waved behind him to get the others to follow him. Then raising his hand up for all of them to see, he signed the word *silent.*

It was fifteen minutes of nerve-racking half jogging, half tiptoeing. The tense atmosphere almost led to Misha accidentally discharging his rifle while some jumped at every little sound. Other than that, they made it to Michael's Rock with no incidents. The enemy still hadn't made themselves known, but he was sure they already had eyes on his team.

The area all around the stone monolith was clear for twenty-five yards. Which made this a spectacular location for pictures, as he was told. Ryder was the first to reach it and he swung his index finger in a circle for everyone to form up. All the operators formed into a huddle, with one about a few feet off to keep watch of the surroundings. Commander Kurepina began relaying orders for them to follow.

"Shut it, I'm trying to hear!" The hushed whispers stopped. "Alright, the commander wants A'Darrion, Fiorenza, and Lek to go through the center. There isn't a lot of cover, so tread carefully. Edward, Olivier, and I will take the right side where the ground starts to rise. Misha, you're charged with distracting The Harpist."

Both the two, three-man cell and the lone wolf split in three directions. Ryder was fine in the large group, but breaking into the smaller teams did rattle him slightly. This enemy was not something he liked to mess around with. There is someone he needed to check in on.

"Hey Evie! You remember the plan, right? When my group gets past the point where the three trees grow from one, you rush to the objective. Don't do anything yourself, we'll tackle it together."

"Don't worry! I have the entire thing memorized." She replied confidently, causing Ryder to chuckle. It was good that she was this confident, not that they had it easy.

The three trees were coming up. The rain had lessened a bit, and he could get a better look through his scope. Ryder swept the area twice, and everything looked clear. As he was taking the scope away from his eye, he caught the slightest shaking of tree branches. Ryder signaled to take cover as assault rifle fire raked the spot his team was just standing. *Shit! That was close!*

Edward and Olivier returned fire as Ryder peeked around the brush. All the shots came from the direction they were heading but kept coming from different angles. Looks like they drew Queen of Hearts, which meant Queen's Guard was probably taking on A'Darrion's team. True to the intel, the toughest enemy was yet to reveal himself, or was at the objective.

The rifle fire was so evenly spread that none of the three dared make a move. Ryder didn't know how Queen of Hearts had their position pinned so accurately. The brush should have provided ample cover, yet somehow their enemy was able to spot them with ease and pin them to this spot. He never underestimated the Queen of Hearts for one second and it still led to this predicament. Ryder almost let out a curse as a round kicked up dirt next to his foot.

If he didn't get his team moving now, the likelihood of the plan failing would increase. Ryder pounded a fist into the dirt, raking his brain for a way around this. Should they double back? Would it be better to charge the center? That would run the risk of the Queen flanking them. His options were limited here and being so close to the objective.

"Commander! We're in a bit of a bind. Ya see anything that I'm not?" Ryder motioned for Edward and Olivier to scoot back to space themselves better.

"Ryder, there is some lower ground to your right. Use that to get around your opponent." He could hear the tension in her voice. It must be pretty rough for her right now.

"Wouldn't that put my group at a major disadvantage?" Ryder flinched as a spray of bullets whizzed overhead.

"There's no time! I can't raise Misha, so you need to move now! Trust me on this." Ryder grumbled at the news. *How did that guy get himself caught this early? He only had one job and somehow managed to bungle it.*

"Team Ryder on the move!" In unison, the three operators sprinted fifty yards to the low ground as a trail of bullets followed. It provided just enough cover that anyone shooting at them had to have expert aim in order to hit them. That little protection didn't mean they were completely safe with all three hugging the ground. There still wasn't any breathing room to return fire, and the gunfire was getting closer and closer.

The sudden crack of a high-powered rifle cut through the sound of the assault rifle. Then the air was silent save for the rain. Ryder cautiously raised his head over the embankment. There was no immediate shooting at him, so the Queen of Hearts was taken down somehow. Ryder ducked his head again just in case he was wrong.

"The way is clear Ryder. Heading towards the objective. Keep up now!" Evie chirped.

"Thanks, I owe you one." Ryder shot a thumbs up towards the clear area in the trees.

"I'll remember that." Evie replied. Ryder just about stood up when Edward forcibly pulled him back down.

"The hell you doin'?!" Ryder swiped the other guy's arm away. Then he saw the terrified look on both Edward and Olivier's faces.

"Just slow down there a second, boss. One more just showed up with the most unfortunate timing." Edward leaned back exasperated. What Ryder saw when he popped his head up made him wince. The last enemy he wanted to see was there, leaning against a tree, pistol twirling in hand... The Harpist.

Evie could see the objective through her scope. It was sitting right out in the open. The only problem was that it was guarded by the toughest opponent anyone could face. What was worse was that her opponent was already looking in her direction. It was hard to tell if he was looking right at her or not. This stare off was deeply unsettling. The hair on her arms stood on end, telling her she should hide.

She took a couple of nervous breaths and ever so slightly, moved the rifle so she could see the other side of the grounds. Ryder said not to go in without him, but at this rate... Moving the rifle back to its original position, that piercing stare greeted her once more. Looks like she would have to pull this off solo. This might work, maybe. Evie fired a shot. *Damn, I missed! Why is he always this good?*

It was the least desirable option, but it looked like she was just going to have to rush him. Evie worked at long range for a reason, close combat not being her strong suit. With her smaller frame and quickness, it could be pulled off. He would have to aim carefully to get her. A perk of being smaller in stature. Evie switched over to her pistol. The sniper rifle would just end up being in the way for this maneuver.

Evie started to slide down the hill, causing a spray of rifle fire. She thought she could at least catch him off guard, but he was ready for her from the start. Once she reached the bottom, she stumbled a bit as she went into a full sprint, just barely staying ahead of the enemy's fire. Evie raised her pistol and began some return fire. Firing a gun while on the move was a lot harder than she thought. Lance made it look so easy. Meanwhile, he remained rooted in place while each of his shots got closer and closer. Evie's pistol clicked when it was empty, which made her focus all of her energy on getting into cover as fast as her legs could carry her. The closest spot of cover was a conveniently parked truck.

Tossing aside the empty magazine, she slid legs first into cover behind the truck. It was a brief respite from the barrage of fire. The objective couldn't be more than twenty yards away now. It might as well be a hundred yards against this guy. Evie wiped sweat from her forehead. It all came down to her whether they came out victorious or not. If those other three buffoons had just backed her up like they were supposed to! Creeping to the other side of the truck, she could feel the intense gaze of her opponent waiting to pounce when she makes this turn. She plastered herself against the muddy truck tire, there's no way she'd be able to take him down. Unless, she didn't have to.

In a split-second decision, Evie tossed her pistol to the other side of the truck where she had started taking cover. Then she jumped out of cover on her end. To her delight, the distraction worked! The gun was pointing in the direction where her pistol had clattered to the ground just beyond the truck, but he was already beginning to swing his rifle in her direction. Everything moved so slowly as Evie reached for her hip. The objective between her and her opponent. The slow draw of the combat knife from its sheath and cocking it back like a hand grenade. She threw her combat knife right before her opponent could squeeze the trigger of his rifle.

Evie heard the round fly just past her ear, felt the heat discharge that followed, reaching out to the objective. Then the next moment the flagpole touched her palm. She let out a few exhausted breaths before shouting in exhilaration. The guy who was so firmly rooted in one spot now a half a step to the right, the rifle held out in one hand. Lance lowered his weapon.

"Good work there, Evie."

"Good job team Kurepina! We won best four out of seven." Lera called out to her operators while doing a series of soft claps. Evie was wooing into the earpiece while the other operators complimented each other on a good day's training. Lera herself was quite relieved after this last match really came down to the wire.

"I'm so glad I didn't have to wait twenty minutes for this round to end." Misha huffed.

"Yeah Misha, I'm real curious. What happened to distracting Heike?" Ryder questioned.

"Well, uh, you see, we kind of ran into each other." Misha laughed.

"The hell does that mean?"

"It means Misha fell into me and I swiftly took action as he was making a joke. I thought I taught him better." Lera listened in on the operators as they continued to ribbing Misha for his rather lackluster performance today. All in all, there was considerable improvement with the less experienced operators. Although, captains didn't get there rank for nothing as Lera had seen firsthand. The others still had a lot of ground to cover. The sound of a door squealed behind her, flooding the communications truck with light.

"Good work, Commander Kurepina."

"You too, Commander Horstmann. Thank you for being my opponent again today." Lera reached out her hand and Helen shook it.

"Anytime. Your grasp on these squads has gotten a lot better. I hope to see this translate into larger units too." Helen complimented as she scrolled through the training footage. "You think you could handle it?"

"I don't think I could achieve the same results. In the end, it just comes down to their execution. They carry out their orders so well. If I had Captain Field, then I probably could have won in four rounds." Lera glanced back at the man on screen.

"Well, the point of this was for you to simulate not having your best troops available to you. Plus, this is good practice for the less experienced to overcome adversity, including you." Helen looked up at the ceiling distantly. "You just never know how much you're going to lose, so keeping discipline and taking on challenges is the only way to make sure you can survive later."

Lera was sure there was a deeper meaning behind those words. She didn't want to pry that from the other commander, so she just let it be. For career soldiers like Horstmann, there had to be plenty of stories, decisions, and defeats that have built up, that weight almost crushing. Yet here she was still in this fight for survival, helping Lera no less.

"Yeah, you're right, still- " A ping in Lera's ear caught her attention and derailed her train of thought. She pointed at her ear to let Helen know someone was on the line. "This is Kurepina. Oh. What can I help you with Major Rikimaru?"

Lera gritted her teeth. This wasn't something she was looking forward to just after finishing a training exercise. Helen noticed her expression and cast a curious glance. She continued to listen to the major give her directions as she fiddled with one of the buttons on her setup.

"Uh-huh. I see, we'll be back shortly." Lera closed the line to her earpiece.

"What's the matter? You look like you ate something bad." Helen swiveled her chair towards Lera and crossed her right leg over her left.

"Intelligence Officer Barrett has requested Captain Field and I for some reason." Lera went back to fiddling with the button.

"Don't let it get to you. It's most likely some routine thing with the emergence of the Terran Revolution Front." Horstmann still didn't ease Lera's mind. As for as she knew, she nor Lance had done anything wrong to come under scrutiny of the onboard intelligence department.

It was at the forefront of her mind as she directed the three squads on cleaning the training grounds. Being able to listen to everyone joke around distracted her just enough to where it wasn't too bothersome. After that, the ride back wasn't engaging, and she found herself back to the matter at hand. There shouldn't be a reason why Barrett was on her and Lance all of a sudden. Not one idea came to Lera as to why. She wasted no time grabbing Lance and heading to the office side of the training complex.

Lera was walking at a faster pace than she normally would. This was something she wanted to get over with, like ripping off a band-aid. Lance was walking a few steps behind her, unlike normal. Ever since the events on Inflar, he and most of the other operators had no problem walking next to her. Even when she did slow her pace down, he wouldn't catch up.

"May I ask why you insist on walking so far behind today?" Lera asked as they reached the designated office.

"Not at all. We had been training for several hours in mud and trees. I really don't smell all to pleasant, so I thought to save you the trouble from that." Lance shrugged.

"I call that an excuse. We've walked battlefields together when there wasn't time to clean up on Verdant Prime." Lera countered.

"This and that are two different environments. We are safe here at a training facility's office where you haven't even broken a sweat, not fighting a battle." Lance pointed out as he crossed his arms, the corners of his mouth raised slightly.

"You make me sound like I'm lazy." Lera complained.

"If I didn't keep catching you doze off all the time it wouldn't come across that way." Lance teased.

"Haha! Very funny! Still, I don't think I was all that great to be around during those times, right?" Lera imitated his stance.

"Nonsense, you always smell nice to me." Caught a little off guard by the comment, Lera didn't know how to reply. Lance knocked on the door, leaving her with that. Usually, like a few moments ago, Lance is rather blunt about things. Something must have him in a good mood of late, he's been rather nice. Lera liked this side of him. A voice beyond the door called them in.

Abigail Barrett stood rigid compared to the figure slouched next to her. This would be the third conversation Lera had with Abigail. Both times were strictly work related, which is how the intelligence officer always did things. Apparently, she is the daughter of the Australian prime minister and came recommended by him. Lera wondered what having that kind of support would be like. The other person was her friend Oskar who, despite his disheveled appearance, looked like he would burst with excitement.

"Thank you for not wasting time in getting here Commander. If you don't mind, I would like to skip formalities and get right into it." Barrett set down a tablet that had several documents preloaded.

"Uh, no, it's fine. I would also like to get this over with. What would the problem be, lieutenant?" Lera asked as she seated herself by the window. Barrett taped the screen of the tablet a few times before answering.

"Not so much a problem, but things need to be sorted out." Barrett switched her attention to Lance. "Operator 212, in this report you submitted, you mentioned something along the lines of 'enemy used telepathic powers'?"

Lance, still standing at attention by the door, looked over at Lera. She nodded her head even though this was news to her. Barrett could be a little more specific on which report it was. By now, it could be any number of them, some written by the vice-captain, Ryder. The operator cleared his throat.

"Yes- "

"That's amazing! Tell me, what is it like? Is it how I always imagined? Can you always hear them? If that's the case, then that could explain the abnormal rate of loss among the operator population!" Oskar interrupted, his lax stature before now perfectly rigid and now a few steps from Lance. Barrett looked at the research head disapprovingly.

"I don't know how you imagined it, or any of that." Lance replied, backing away from the other man.

"Calm down Oskar," Lera laughed," why all the excitement?"

"Precisely, for all we know, the operator could have had a mental breakdown and submitted a false report. Which we won't know now." Barrett put her hands on her hips then mumbled something only she could hear.

"Apologies but remember how we haven't been able to crack the code on the Vekros' language? I believe that the key is in the telepathic ability they have." Oskar said all in one breath, finally backing away from Lance.

"Hmm. How did I overlook that in the report?" Lera groaned, putting a hand to her forehead. She had an idea why; it was the same night she fell asleep in the living room of the operators' building.

"Either way, 212, please go with our lead R&D officer for further analysis." The two men started towards the door. "I'd like to talk to you about these documents here. Athena Project."

Lera heard a boot scuff the ground. Turning back towards the door, Lance was stopped mid-step. His jaw clenched, and his eyes had an unnatural coolness to them.

"Please 212, you're not needed here." Barrett said annoyed as her finger started to tap against the tablet again. Lance glanced back at Lera before closing the door behind him. Lera stared at the closed door for a second longer. *What was that look? He looked a little distressed at the mention of Athena. How connected was he to this?*

"Tell me how much you know." Barrett's tapping increased. Right, Barrett is here now. Lance would have to wait for the time being.

"All that was sent to me. The circumstances of Athena Corps' founding early in the war. Some of the important figures of the organization. Dr. Marilyn Farver stood out to me. I haven't delved too much into it, but I know it has to do with the operators." Lera explained. The intelligence officer finally stopped tapping.

"How do you know?" Barrett scrutinized as she made a couple swipes on the screen.

"It doesn't explicitly say. There was something along the lines of optimization of human based weapons. Which could be a misleading term... It's a hunch." Barrett didn't look convinced by Lera's answer.

"Did you know those documents are Grade Five. Ninety-nine percent of the EEN isn't allowed to lay eyes on those documents, yet you did it with no regard for the consequences. You could be court-martialed and put in federal prison for the rest of your life." The last sentence hung in Lera's mind. She did know that risk, but it was all to better understand Lance and her soldiers she commanded.

"Do what you must. I did it to better help my troops." There was no choice for her. She had made up her mind a long time ago. Lera looked up defiantly, expecting to be berated by the EEN regulation. Instead, the intelligence officer looked at her inquisitively.

"Calm down, Commander. I have no intention of reporting this." Barrett sat across from Lera. "To be fair, this Athena Corps thing has also piqued my interest. Something being hidden from the rest of the military and world leaders is suspicious. I want you to work with me is what I'm trying to ask."

"Huh? Wait! What was all that about Grade Five and federal prison?" Lera asked quickly.

"I was just pointing out the risks involved and testing your mindset on the issue. You passed by the way, though not for the reason I would have expected." Abigail flipped through her tablet. "We'll end it here and meet up again another time to discuss this set of documents. If you receive more, then please send those to me too."

Lera stared at Abigail in confusion. How did she even get the documents in the first place? Why was she also interested in Athena Corps? Whatever the case, it looks like it was something to come up later. For now, she better go check on her operators.

Chapter 1

Kanto-IV

Noah Stone leaned back in his chair watching the footage sent after the training exercise. Ivy and Shi were busy scrutinizing every minor detail. He already had a few ideas on how to optimize each operator's strengths. That being said, he also couldn't underestimate the unpredictability of their actions. That was why they did these, to hone each operator's skills and teamwork, and rectify any troublesome behavior. Noah had to be patient since the other two handlers enjoyed doing in-depth analysis of each operator's performance.

"Do you guys know which squads are the top ones in the southern theatre?" Noah asked to break the long silence, running a hand through his red hair. Shi lifted her head and stared at him blankly.

"Where is this coming from?" Ivy flicked her eyes up at him for a second.

"Only speeding up the process, I've already came up with a few ideas to implement after this exercise and I know that you'll eventually reach the same conclusion." Noah rested his chin on his hand. "Are you interested yet?"

"I'm going to ignore your rather unprofessional comment." Ivy replied curtly.

"Hmm, was it Snow Squall?" Shi guessed.

"Believe it or not, but the top three squads are yours truly." Noah smiled as he motioned towards the tablet in front of him.

"No way! Our squads did that?" Ivy leaned it to get a better look at the contents on screen.

"I assure you, yes. My connections within Athena as well as the other handlers are solid. They even had the gall to ask whether there was any room for the favored trainees. Meanwhile, other squads had been trying to transfer to the Moskva to no avail." Noah informed with a sly smile. "I flatly refused the extra manpower, not that we don't need it, and the handlers' requests have been denied."

"I'm not surprised by any of *your* actions. What is surprising is command not forcefully transferring squads to us. If we consider the resounding success we have had since the commander took over, it makes you wonder what they're planning." Ivy looked off to her bottom left, deep in thought.

"Where do we stand as a whole?" Shi asked.

"Top twenty from what I saw. The squads in the northern theatre are always in the most intense of the fighting." Noah replied rather disappointed. Despite not failing a single mission for the past nine months or so, it only landed them in the top twenty. He would very much like to talk to this orchestrator of the rankings. That top ten was just out of reach. The top ten always got the best equipment and given preference when picking new recruits.

Not long ago, Noah had the chance to snag a talent that was generational. This kid was going to be better than him, which is high praise if anyone asked the other handlers. That was Shi's very own Revenant. Except, some idiot enticed him just a little bit more. If he had known that Revenant had lost so many of his squads, Noah would have snatched him up quickly. That information was somehow kept from him when it did happen.

"I begrudgingly have to give the commander credit. With us being able to focus solely on training the squads makes each one of them capable of being captain's themselves." Ivy frowned.

"Are you not happy with their possible promotions?"

"That's not it Stonewall. It's a good thing. It shows we are excellent drill sergeants, but I could say that I'd miss them if it did happen." Ivy went back to her tablet.

"It's not like we were going to tell them, of course. We don't want to swell their heads with delusions of grandeur." Noah gave Spiritwalker a sidelong glance. "How very unlike you to compliment that little girl, hmm?"

"Shut up! Even I have to recognize talent when I see it!" Noah scoffed at Ivy's statement.

"Here," Ivy flipped the tablet and slid it in his direction, "don't ask how I got this, but I've never seen anything like it."

Noah lifted the tablet, giving Ivy a doubtful look before he went to read the screen. Some basic background info, with details of her past and other nonsense. Combat sims were pretty high compared to others that he'd seen. Noah could give her that much, then he froze at the last couple of pages. *There's no way that this was possible. Our commander- that little princess- achieved that?!*

Noah wanted to jump in excitement, just barely able to control himself by bouncing his leg. He couldn't believe how lucky they were to have such an asset that was all theirs. Noah burst into laughter, no longer able to contain himself. This caused the other two to jump in surprise. Seeing this file puts a lot of things in perspective. It made sense why the commander was in such an awkward position in terms of military placement.

"I have no idea what you're going crazy about, but at least you see I'm not lying." Ivy pouted.

"I know. I know." Noah went to wipe tears from his eyes. "The two keys to changing the war are right in our laps ladies. This is something that we cannot screw up."

"What's your plan?" Shi asked, rubbing her eyes as she yawned.

"We continue what we're doing now, but I want to personally train Revenant. If that is alright with you Rose?" A fire was now lit under Noah that he thought was extinguished. After seeing so many of his comrades die, the war that kept on going, things were finally coming together. The EEN had lost sixty percent of its original forces, but that was rebounding. Technology was finally catching up with the needs of the conflict. And it all swirled around those two. *It looks like I have to get serious from here on out.*

"I trust your judgement, but please don't break my operator." Shi yawned.

"Can you break something that is already broken? It's not going to be a problem."

It was a bad idea for this R&D guy to choose such a small room to conduct this debriefing. Typically, his superiors withheld their questions until the end. The man in front of him interjected any chance he could. Lance had almost completely lost his patience and would have knocked the guy on the side of the head. What prevented him from doing so was Commander Kurepina's disappointment, and the assistant that was seated next to the man. She kept Schneider on track, for the most part.

The assistant wore the same thing as her department head, Schneider. She wrote everything that Lance described down on a notepad with any comments her boss had. Her hair was in something the commander called a "braid", except this one was circled around her head. She was normal enough besides willingly staying around this guy.

"Oh, Novanna, please finish this up for me. I've been called back by Corey about the scheduled reactor test." Oskar straightened himself out as he got up from the chair.

"Not a problem. We were almost done anyway." Novanna replied. Oskar looked over Novanna's shoulder at the notes, muttering to himself. She then waited for the door to close and the steps to recede before looking back at Lance. "I have no questions for you, so feel free to go."

"Are you sure? Is it alright with that guy?" Lance stood up, glad that he could finally get away from this small room.

"Yeah. I could tell that you were feeling his attention to detail. Mister Schneider can be... overwhelming to be around. Trust me on this, his intentions are good. You won't find a less judgmental person." Novanna followed him out. "You know that reactor test is just a ploy. In reality he's working on a little side project for the captain's daughter."

"Why are you telling me this?" Lance grumbled.

"You just get along with the poor kid. Both you and Oskar seem to enjoy the company of kids so I thought it would help understand him a little." The assistant replied.

"I prefer not to be compared to him."

"Apologies then. Anyway, my turn is here. The stairs at the end of the hall lead back to the first floor." Novanna directed before she walked away but turned around for a few seconds. "If you ever need support, we'll answer that call, Mr. Revenant."

Lance nodded slightly. He appreciated the sentiment, but he already knew where to go from here. There was also no way he'd ever ask a favor from that aggravating desk jockey. He didn't need them. Lance wanted to go up three floors where he left the commander to see if she was still up in the offices, instead, he decided not to do that in favor of getting a shower. The rest of the squads had finished up by now, giving him the area to himself. It gave him time to think, which he did a lot nowadays. After a few minutes of searching, he made it to the locker room.

As he thought, this room and the adjoining one were empty. It would mean his squads were either waiting for him somewhere else or had gone back to the shuttles. Lance got undressed and neatly folded the dirty fatigues in the bin. He doubted anyone else was going to be in here today, but just in case, he closed the curtain. No need to scare some trainee with the multitude of scars across his body.

Lance's ability allowed him to dodge almost anything as long as he had line of sight. Add in the experience he had; Lance was virtually untouchable. It didn't mean he was invincible. There had been too many close calls, the evidence being those scars. He couldn't count all the times he fell from far heights or was nicked by stray rounds that were painted across him like a painter would a canvas. Whether they were on his back, arms, or legs, they were ugly reminders. He scrubbed roughly over those surfaces trying to remove the stains of his past failures, only to swing at the curtain behind him in frustration when they were still there. Lance leaned one hand against the wall while the other held his face. Looking through the cracks between his fingers, the scars on his outstretched arm mocking him. He rolled his eyes with a heavy sigh. *How'd I even live this long? It's not fair that I'm still here while the others... They deserve to be here instead of me.*

Lance leaned back, letting the water stream down his chest. The weight of his black hair trying to pull him back into the depths of despair. Compared to the rain, the hot water felt so much better. It reminded him of something that was there at the edge of his mind. No matter how hard he thought about it, he could never reach that image. An outline, no- two figures he couldn't make out. A weak, sorrowful voice called out. *Come back! Please! Don't leave!* The image faded away. As he stood there, Lance realized he had reflexively reached out. Something in his chest was close to breaking, and he wanted to scream out.

Ping

"Lance." He breathed heavily.

"Yo, the commander is ready to leave when you get here." Ryder informed.

"She knows she can contact me anytime, right?"

"Oh, she does. She doesn't want to bother you since you're showering." Lance could hear another higher pitched voice in the background.

"I don't see a problem."

"*Of course you don't.* Just hurry I guess; she's saying to leave you be. We'll be waiting like I said." The other end went silent. Shutting off the water, Lance hurriedly changed into an extra pair of black fatigues worn by most of the Moskva's defense crew. He got it about a month or so at his door with a note from Master Sergeant Auch saying she expected assistance if they were to somehow be boarded. The gold captain's insignia stood out against the black. As Lance was leaving the locker room, another soldier bumped into him and fell to the floor.

"Sorry Captain! I couldn't move out of the way fast enough." The girl quickly got to her feet and saluted; the woman's voice was lower from what he expected from her height. Lance, unsure of what to do exactly, gave a half-hearted salute in return. Her dark brown hair was short, longer at the top and faded at the sides. Her brown eyes, like a puppy's, looked up at him expectantly. Lance began to walk away before she called out to him. "Sir, please wait!"

"Sir, I'm actually a little lost. May I ask for some assistance if it isn't too much trouble?" Lance nodded to the door, and she came up beside him. "Thank you, sir. I was supposed to report to my new assignment, but the person I was looking for wasn't where the front desk said they'd be."

"I can't guarantee that I know them, but I'll help you find them. What's the name?" Lance asked as the soldier opened the door for him. From her mannerisms, she seemed to be a rookie. That crushing anxiety they have masked by false confidence.

"Kurepina, sir." The girl replied. Lance stopped and turned to face her.

"Wait. What's your name?" Lance asked.

"Sorry, where is my discipline. Sergeant Emma Sytnikova. Sir!" Sytnikova clicked the heels of her boots together.

"Sergeant? Shouldn't you be part of a squad?" Lance inquired as they continued on.

"I am, but I'm on special assignment. At least that's what I was told." Sytnikova stiffened like she was bracing to be reprimanded. Getting confused for a navy officer was getting annoying.

"Relax Sergeant, I'll take you to her." Lance tried to put some feeling into the words. It looked like it worked when Sytnikova relaxed her shoulders.

"Thank you again, Sir! May I ask your name?"

"Reve- " Lance paused. An image of the commander popped into his mind. The wet behind the ears commander who didn't recognize the operators in front of her, insisting that they were more than just numbers.

"Lance Field." Lance imitated what he saw Kurepina do in these situations. He reached out his hand and she returned the handshake.

"Nice to make your acquaintance, Captain Field." Lance listened to Sytnikova recount her basic training and how different it must be from the officer's academy. He understood the basic training part, though he'd rather not think about those times. They paused inside the door that led out to the flight pad. Lance wasn't quite ready to step out there just yet.

"Sytnikova, before we head out there. Will you do everything in your power to protect your commander?" Lance asked with a heavy gaze. The sergeant looked at him like he was dumb.

"Of course I will. Superior officer or not, I'd do anything I could. But why exactly are you asking, Sir?"

"Just think of it as a personal request." Lance paused mid-step. "Don't mention this to her either. Let's go."

Lera watched the time change on her handheld yet again. She hadn't a clue as to what was keeping him from getting here. Lance was punctual with everything. So, she was starting to get frustrated with the one time he wasn't. It wasn't just her; the ground crew didn't want to spend time here if they didn't have to either. The operators all huddled together; lost in some conversation she wasn't invited to. The doors finally opened with one they were waiting for.

"It's sure not like to fall behind now, Captain. I'm sure everything was fine, right?" Lera noticed the different uniform used by the navy personnel he was wearing. The Officer's suited him too.

"Sorry, Commander. Didn't mean for it to happen." Lance replied as he stopped a few feet from her. Then someone else appeared from behind him unexpectedly.

"Wait, Captain. You didn't say she was your superior too." The girl looked at him with surprise. Lance shrugged like it wasn't important, then took his place next to Lera. Lera observed the newcomer who was somehow on friendly terms with Lance.

"Name and rank soldier. What's your business for being here?" Lera ordered. The girl snapped to attention quickly.

"Emma Sytnikova, sergeant. Reporting to Commander Kurepina for assignment." Sytnikova said from a rehearsed line. The thing is, Lera never requested for help, let alone a single sergeant. Which begged the question. Why was she here in the first place?

"Say, who sent you here?" Lera asked. Sytnikova's stature slackened as she began to think. Lera glanced at Lance who again, just shrugged.

"Umm, Alice? Alma? Abby? Oh, Abigail Barrett!" Emma snapped her fingers as she found the answer. *Say what?!*

"That's certainly an interesting surprise. Welcome aboard the Moskva, Sergeant Syntikova." After that, Lera, the sergeant, and the operators boarded the awaiting shuttle.

During the flight back to the Moskva, Emma Sytnikova retold her entire story of how she ended up here. Lera was too busy in her own mind to even listen to her speak to the operators. As nice as the sergeant was, Lera wasn't fond of Barrett deciding she could make personnel decisions without consulting her first. She watched her operators as they excitedly watched the docking sequence like kids.

After working with them for the past eight months or so, they felt more like a tight knit group. Although Lera still didn't know where she fit among them. Was she still just another commander to them? Could they be more than just commander and operator? Sure, they treated her with respect, and they messed around with her the same they did to each other. That still didn't do enough to assuage Lera's doubts.

The ramp opened when they finished docking. Lance was the first one off, so Lera tried to catch up with him. Right before she could get to his side, Emma Sytnikova jumped in front of her and talked to Lance. Figuring it was just a question, Lera followed behind until they finished.

"So, the guy with the big scar just said you guys were operators! You really had me fooled there Mister Rev." Emma exclaimed, hitting Lance in the back.

"I wasn't trying to. You just never asked." Lance replied ignoring the contact.

"I would have, but you were just too nice. Very unlike the stories I was told."

"How so?" Lance questioned.

"My drill sergeant always talked down about you. Saying that all you're good for is killing and being an asshole, but I'm glad that isn't the case." Emma lightly punched Lance's arm.

"I was just emulating what my commander would do. Having someone with a good opinion of me isn't a bad thing either." Lance pushed Emma away lightly. Lera was confused as to why Lance was acting the way he was. She had never seen him act so friendly with someone, if she could call that being friendly. He hadn't really been like this since the incident with the Terran Revolution Front. While Emma walked away, another person butted in front of Lera. This one she was more than fine with.

"Lance! You're back!" Oliviana ran into Lance as he squatted down. She hugged him like a younger sibling would to their older sibling. This time, his demeanor totally took a one eighty from his normal self.

"You look like you're in high spirits today." Lance commented as he messed her hair.

"It's my birthday tomorrow silly." Oliviana giggled. "Don't tell me you forgot."

"Of course not. You'll be twelve, right?" Lance smiled lightly. The little girl looked at him with sparkles in her eyes.

"Yep! I almost caught up to you, see." The girl claimed as she tried to flex. Lera couldn't help but giggle to herself at the ridiculous display.

"Umm, I think you have a little while to go." Lance teased, which brought on a barrage of punches he easily blocked. He put her arms down to her side.

"I'm giving this to you a day early, since you've been working so hard." Lance reached towards his back pocket and pulled something out and handed it to Oliviana.

"Wow! Do they match yours?" Oliviana asked as her face lit up with joy. Lance pulled out his dog tags from around his neck.

"Sure do. Make sure to always wear them so I can find you." Lance told her. Oliviana put the dog tags around her neck.

"I will! Let's play sticks now!" Oliviana held out two fingers.

"Alright, let's see if you can beat me this time." Lance got in the same position as his little opponent. This was the only good thing about Lance being away for an extended period of time. It took him a long time to settle back into relaxation. When Oliviana was around, it caused so many entertaining interactions between those two, like they always had been siblings.

She kind of wished he was like this all the time. Lance looked so carefree, like this war was all a dream. That he was just an older brother returning from a hard day's work. Introducing his family to… Lera shook her head. That wasn't something she should be thinking about. What was in front of her was enough.

That tiny thought still remained. If there was never a war, would Lance still be orphan, or would he have a family? What would he have been like? Where would he be, and would she have ever met him? If they did meet, then was it possible... But then she would miss the one in front of her now, however distant he was. Lera had worked too hard to get to know this Lance, so another could never work.

"Hello? Earth to Commander?" Came the voice of her personal aide waving a hand in front of her.

"Ah! Major?! How long have you been there?" Lera asked as she let go of the strand of hair she had been stroking.

"About a minute. You were really deep in thought." Major Rikimaru remarked, repositioning his cap. "It must have been something nice with the expression you had."

"No. I was just excited to get back to work." Lera lied watching one of her operators do the exact opposite.

"Oh, well then, the Captain has requested you to his office. Looks to be another big operation coming up." Rikimaru informed in a hushed voice, leaning in to make sure only Lera heard.

"Thank you, Major. I guess I should get to that then." Lera took one last glance over at Lance and Oliviana before she left. There would be some time later to share company.

Remember. Stay out of sight. Don't let your quarry detect your presence, good. Stealthily approach, like a specter you are. Ready. Set. Strike!

Misha jumped out from behind a box and ran up on his target. Everything was going like he thought it would. She wasn't going to know what hit her. Misha reached out for the accessory on her head. His world suddenly went topsy-turny and his face was pushed into the floor, his arm twisted above him.

"Ooww! Ow! Ow! I yield!" Misha cried out trying to raise his head only a little. His arm was forcefully pushed down.

"Hmph! Serves you right. Did you even try?" Heike raised her boot and stomped next to Misha's head. "If this was real combat, you'd be dead."

Misha got up and dusted himself off while Heike left. The three witnesses to the ordeal were her very own subordinates. None of them looked surprised by the outcome. Edward at least helped him up.

"You had a good try. I'd say better than your showing earlier." Fiorenza gave a back-handed compliment.

"I planned all that today, not really, but kind of." Misha patted Edward's shoulder as thanks for helping. "I didn't have my A-game, so that means the next mission means I'll be like dangerous as a jaguar."

"We sure hope so." Olivier grinned.

"What's your plans for the day?" Misha asked. The three members of Fenrir looked at each other.

"Well, we planned on getting on the flight simulators again. You guys may be done with training for today, but we have to keep up on our flight skills." Fiorenza stated, the other two nodding in agreement.

"It's part of the reason Heike was a little rough with you just now. I'm sure she's exhausted and wants to rest." Edward looked worriedly in the direction Heike went. "I really don't know how she can continue on with all that she has going on."

"Well, with Lance here now, she's gotten a lot better." Olivier mentioned. Edward put a fist into his hand in agreement.

"You're right, Olivier. We should have Lance train with Heike on the simulator too." Edward declared.

"I second that." Misha raised his hand.

"How did you two come up with that conclusion?" Fiorenza asked to herself.

"Hey! Can I go with you guys? There isn't much for me to do now, unless Chika finds me of course." Misha clasped two hands together in a plea.

"I like that idea, makes things more lively. Let's go kill some virtual Veks!" Edward cheered as Misha followed happily. Fiorenza and Olivier exchanged exasperated expressions before following in turn.

Lance played a game with Oliviana for a little while, beating her every time, much to the little girl's dismay. Like every other time, Doctor Edwards came looking for her. After some encouragement, Lance convinced Oliviana to go with the doctor with the promise of seeing her later. When all was said and done, he found himself alone. Commander Kurepina was with him. He had to guess that she had something come up.

There was one thing he wanted to get out of the way. Besides Heike, the other two captains and the vice-captain were going to go over squad tactics with the handlers. With the ever-changing conditions of a battlefield, having a clear idea of what to do when was invaluable. Lance himself wasn't much help when it came to that. The only way he did things was to get right into the thick of fighting. The faster he took out the Vekros, the faster the mission was completed. For obvious reasons, the other operators couldn't do that. He still had his misgivings working with a team, but Lance finally thought that it wasn't such a terrible thing.

"Lance! Wait up!" Lance turned around to both Chika and Rene holding hands.

"Are you already going to meet with the handlers?" Rene asked.

"Yeah. I just want to get it done and over with." Lance began to walk again with the other two now joining him. He ignored their, well, whatever it was called that couples behaved. They swung their intertwined hands happily like they were the only two in this ship. Whispering to each other and laughing every so often.

The area chosen to have the meeting was the officer's lounge. Lance would have preferred a room that was quieter and out of sight from the regs. That was one thing he had not gotten used to yet. Integrating with the rest of the military had its share of complaints, both from the operators and regs when it first happened. Now both parties mostly got along.

Lance, Rene, and Chika were the first to arrive. He chose a table that was towards the back while the other two captains went and grabbed a few food items. Minutes later, the three handlers took their seats across from the captains. As every conversation would start out, the exchange of greetings, how the day was going, and other minor details. Stonewall did most, if not all, of the talking. Eventually, even his motor for conversation subsided, and now they could get this thing done.

"After today's set of matches, there isn't a whole lot that we can improve on," Ivy was working her tablet, moving from one circled and scribbled on photo to another, pointing out minor things, "I've noticed that a lot of the basics of been neglected of late. Not having awareness of surroundings, lack of discipline, and stuff like that. Those need to be rectified or it could lead to someone getting killed."

"Right. We'll have to talk it over with them and get it sorted it out right away." Rene acknowledged. Lance sat with his hands clasped in front of his face, eyes closed.

"Rose, Spiritwalker, and I were just discussing this earlier," Stonewall paused, causing Lance to open his eyes. The handler was eyeing Lance, which he returned with a cold gaze that didn't faze the smile on Stonewall. "Revenant, you have the honor of being personally sculpted by yours truly, which I mean trained."

"Not going to happen." Lance replied curtly. The very quiet, half-asleep Rose shot halfway across the table, causing a cup to fall and spill its contents.

"What makes you think that you deny such a gesture?" Rose asked impatiently.

"Can I say that I don't want his help?" Lance suggested.

"You could, but that doesn't mean anything with me." Rose rolled her eyes and went back to her chair. "I don't have the patience to deal with you right now, so this is an order, not a request. Understand?"

"Affirmative."

"Frankly, Lance. Catching the attention of *the* top operator should garner more respect." Rene whispered.

"*Former* operator." Lance said out loud.

"Let me strike a deal." Stonewall gave a mischievous look. "You either work with me, or your little princess commander is going to hear of your tantrum."

"Have it your way." Lance grumbled. It wasn't that he minded, he'd rather not be around Stonewall. The handler was too bright for a guy who's been around and seen some things. It was worse having Commander Kurepina placate things when she already had so much to do. Lance also didn't want to look uncooperative, so there's that. Just like that, the meeting was over.

Lera waited for Captain James to finish reading whatever he was scrolling through. She had to wonder if anything good happened to him recently. He looked a lot happier than he normally did. It was something she normally didn't get to see. She listened to him hum a tune to himself. If Lera was in his situation, she would rather have a cushy desk job at EENHQ than be stuck on a ship. It seemed, just like sea-based sailors, the allure of space was too much to stay away from.

"Captain. You seem to be in a good mood today." Lera started off the conversation, still standing in relaxed attention.

"I am. I watched the young captain play with Oliviana. I don't remember the last time I saw her smile like that." Captain James lifted up a picture from his desk and smiled weakly at it.

"It's good to see that there's something good coming out of that. Both of you have had it hard. The operators and I are always ready to help when you need it." Lera smiled.

"I'll keep that in mind, Commander. Right, before I forget," Captain James reached into his desk drawer and took out an expensive-looking bottle. "I know it's early, but I should give this to you before the next operation."

"Thank you, Captain. Can I ask what this is for?" Lera took and studied the bottle. It was an alcoholic beverage of some kind, most definitely an expensive one too. She couldn't even read the name on the bottle. "You know I'll only be nineteen... It's a birthday present. Is it already that time back home?"

"Yeah, July starts next week, and your birthday the week after that." Blake James laughed. "Usually, youths like you count down the days to your twenty-first. It shows how burled your head has been in your work, not that that is a bad thing."

"Why this specifically?" Lera inquired as she set the bottle off to this side.

"I do this for all of my XOs for their first birthday in the military. It's brandy, something that British naval officers would give to their crew after a hard-fought win. This may not be a victory of any sorts, but this is a way to show my appreciation for choosing to come fight a war when you don't have to." James replied slightly amused.

"Thank you again. I would have forgotten about it if not for this. I'll send it home on the next mail run." Lera wondered what her mom would think when this thing came in the mail. Her dad better be the one who picks it up.

"So, has the top brass determined where we'll strike next?" Lera pivoted the conversation back to why she was here.

"Correct. We're retaking the core world of Kanto-IV and the surrounding system." A blue screen popped up between them, showing the planet and the system that encompassed it. "Tell me what you know from these graphics."

"Why, Sir?"

"Just tell me what you know, and you might can an answer." Captain James leaned back and placed his hands behind his head.

Lera got to work studying the graphics. She started off by going over what presence the Vekros had. The Vekros fleet wasn't nearly as big as the first one she had encountered. There was only a carrier, three battleships, seven cruisers, and fifteen destroyers. No fifteen-kilometer super ships this time. The enemy fleet may be small, but it was still an even match between them and the EEN fleet. The X-factor was the EENS Moskva, the ship she was on now.

From the last round of intelligence that was displayed, the fleet was set up in a classic formation. The carrier, most likely the flagship, was centered around the three battleships. The cruisers and destroyers surrounded those four ships to create a network of strong point defense coordination. A no-fly zone, so to speak. That wasn't going to break up without a good reason, or if the enemy leader underestimated his opponents.

The ground presence was overwhelming. A force of ten million was holding all of the key positions on the planet. Unlike the enemy on Verdant Prime, these ones would be dug in and well equipped for an assault. It will be an uphill battle for the five million soldiers being deployed to retake Kanto-IV. Although Lera had confidence that her three operator squads could easily take out over two million Vekros over the span of the operation.

What didn't sit right was why the Vekros wanted to keep this planet so badly. That was the real question that needed to be answered. The ecology was similar to that of Earth, though most planets that the EEN had colonized were like that. The planet itself was a lot smaller than most, almost like a moon. Then it hit her. Kanto-IV was rich in mineral deposits. It was a heavily industrialized planet pumping out billions each quarter before war came on its doorstep. Lera's father had a stake in one of the companies before the war if she remembered correctly.

Lera recited all the information she thought was important. Captain James listened intently, asking questions to get a better understanding of the situation and to see her thought process. After she had finished, he began writing things down on a notepad. Lera waited for him to bring this meeting to a close.

"Tell me XO. How would you handle this combat situation?" James got out of his chair and stared out of the viewport that was behind him. Lera took a second to get the gears in her mind to move again.

"The enemy fleet is strong for what few ships they have. It consists of all new-gen ships. Reaper-class destroyers, Rapture-class cruisers, Minotaur-class battleships, and an Aries-class carrier." Lera paused as she began to play around with a few scenarios in her head. Referencing other fleet engagements that stood out to her. "Our first priority is to protect our carriers. They are the lifeblood of a fleet, which means that half our strength will already be situated in a defensive role. Using the Second Assault Group, I'd use them as a screening force to draw away the enemy destroyers. Once that happens, the First Assault Group battleships will engage at range while cruisers provide point-defense cover."

"I'll leave the Third Assault Group as a reserve force to either provide support, or to protect the ground transports. Meanwhile, the Moskva will take out the enemy carrier." It was rather crude to Lera, but it was the best she could come up with being asked on the spot.

"I see the merits of this, but why have the flagship unescorted go after the enemy carrier?" Captain James asked as he messed with a chart on the board.

"The Moskva is fast enough to keep pace with the carrier if it attempts to make a run for it. On top of that, the weapons systems are more than capable of taking on enemy spacecraft or larger ships. And if we need to, we could easily pull back ourselves since we're faster than the enemy's big guns." Lera responded.

"What if the Vekros send all their ships against the second group? What's your response?" James wrote something on the chart. Lera had started to get a feeling that this was some kind of test.

"First group will support the second while the third takes on the vanguard role. The essence of the plan doesn't change." James stopped writing and looked at her from the corner of his eye.

"Meaning?"

"Figuring that the enemy flagship is one of the capital ships, if I'm wrong about it being the carrier, our carriers' spacecraft will focus on crippling the enemy battleships so ours can land their shots. The third group's destroyers could catch the enemy carrier with their superior speed. Either way, the focus would be to decimate the Vekros chain of command, leaving the rest of their fleet in shambles without the ability to coordinate cohesively." Lera explained. The captain continued on with the questions and the what ifs. What would she do if reinforcements arrived? What if the intel was wrong? She answered each one with something that would counter whatever scenario he came up with.

"Final question. How many ships do you think you'd lose with this plan?" James asked, finishing whatever he was doing on the board. That's the part Lera wanted to avoid, but she should have expected something along those lines.

"Ideally, zero. Realistically, I would say at most, twelve." Lera replied. The captain raised his eyebrows.

"That is rather optimistic, wouldn't you say XO?" Lera knew it sounded crazy. Barring any unforeseen development and basing it on current Vekros strategy, the scenario she came up with played out that way. Even with all the other scenarios he had thrown at her, as long as the fleet stuck with the plan, with some variation, it would still end the same way.

"It isn't if you think about it. The Vekros know they are outnumbered here, but they rely on their overwhelming firepower or numbers. They have one of those keys. They'll commit to taking out where our strength lies, the carriers." James gestured for her to continue. "We won't give them a chance with our fake out and vanguard. It's pretty clear that the Vekros don't yet have an idea what the Moskva is capable of, therefore, they will largely leave it alone. This allows us to cut the head of the snake before it can bite."

"I applaud you Kurepina. The plan you came up with is way more efficient than the one Command drew up." Captain James praised. "I knew I could count on you."

"What do you mean, Sir?" Lera appreciated the praise, but why had he asked her in the first place. She was just some XO. How could her plan be better than the one that the top military strategists in Command came up with?

"Simple. I want you to take the reins on this one." James returned to his chair where he instinctively reached for his cigar.

"Oh, well of cours- Wait! Me take command?!" Lera shouted, placing her hands on the desk.

"Yes, in five days. Don't worry too much, I'll be there to provide guidance and support, or take over if things get to hot. I think it is the perfect opportunity to test your mettle. If I heard from a friend right, you've garnered the attention of The Chief." James told her. Lera didn't know what to believe. That she was commanding a battle or that she caught the attention of The Chief himself.

"I won't let you down, Captain." Lera replied eagerly. Captain James grinned at her enthusiasm.

"I know you won't. Whatever happens, you'll come out on top." Captain James encouraged. Lera left the room in a bubble of excitement. Her steps had a little more pep than they did before. Today was just a good day and she was going to finish it off with a sweet treat. In five days' time, it was time for her to prove herself once more.

Chapter 2

Fenrir's Bout

Out of all the operators aboard the ship, they were the only four in the room, and her squad at that. The other two squads for reasons that didn't concern Heike were absent. Since it was only her squad, she was disappointed as they were dull people to be around. Heike turned up the volume on her headphones. She'd rather not have to hear her own subordinates joke around; or listen to that oaf of a handler.

Heike stretched herself out in an attempt to get all of the aches and pains out. The day's exercise wasn't exactly tough by any stretch, but physical activity at those spurts of intensity and length got to her this time. Her two male subordinates, they were more than just poor performance. She easily dispatched both of them after she had taken care of that pesky infiltrator. The third one... Ryder. Well, it made sense why Lance had picked him as his second. He actually made Heike break a sweat to take him out. She never had to work that hard against anyone that wasn't Lance, Rene, Chika, or the handlers.

"Ahem! Heike, please get off the table, it's not a bed." Came a feminine voice as her headphones were lifted. *What impudent witch-*

When Heike opened her eyes, it was the commander that was standing above her. As much as she would have liked to ignore Kurepina, Lance gave a strict order to follow whatever the commander said. On top of that, if Lance had been in this room, he would know exactly what she was thinking which could have led to some sparring, or just an earful later. *I guess I'm safe this time.*

"Ughhh, fine, but only if you sing to me." Heike crossed her fingers. She had waited for this moment ever since Lance told her that the commander used to sing. It was something interesting that most people couldn't do, and she wanted to know if the commander was any good.

"I don't know who told you that, but I refuse." Lera shot a hard glance at the giggling Fiorenza, who started pulling on the collar of her fatigues nervously.

"It was a joke. You probably can't sing anyway." Heike taunted. She hoped that it would stir something up.

"A joke? Last time I checked, this was a military vessel and not a circus. At least a clown knows when to end its act." Lera countered. Heike was surprised that the commander could come up with counters that quickly. The only other one was Lance.

"I concede." Heike turned down the volume the same time a good song came on. Too bad she couldn't pause it right now.

"Good. Now it's time for your briefing." Lera began as she walked to the front of the room. The only reason Fenrir was chosen was because they were the only squad that has been in space combat, or low gravity flight to better explain it. The other two squads were going to stay behind on this one while Fenrir lead the fighter escort that would protect the bombers.

The targets were the enemy battleships. It was a pretty ballsy move only using fifty spacecraft to achieve that goal. The point defense cannons were no joke. Trying to dodge incoming fire from them and protect the bombers from enemy fighters as well as not getting tangled by them herself, it was going to be a handful. The Vekros battleship's defenses against spacecraft weren't on par with a cruiser, but they were not to be trifled with. Heike still liked this plan. This was the type of danger that got her blood pumping.

If the battleships were taken out swiftly enough, there was a chance to go after the carrier as well. Not that the fighters would be able to do match but be an annoyance. It could be enough of a distraction to allow the bombers to resupply and take the carrier out. Then it would be a simple task of mopping up whatever Vekros are left. After that, it was going to the surface and starting the ground portion of the operation. Operation Genesis.

Commander Kurepina told them that they had three hours to prepare. The fleet had been on the move since they returned from Yire's surface and were already making the final approach to the Kanto system. That's how it goes when most of the territory had been taken, leaving little room for rest sometimes. Heike knew she was known to be indifferent to where they went or what they do, and she had to admit that there was some truth to that. Contrary to what people think they know, she always made sure to read up on their target location when she could. That made her in more need of rest, so that had to prove the other fools wrong in some way.

Of course, all the other teams on the Moskva were ready, leaving the rooms empty for Fenrir squad to change. Heike stared blankly at the Flight Suit Survival Apparatus, or FSSA. It was exactly as it sounds. This thing that only the Research Bureau understood, could keep a pilot alive for a week if their fighter was disabled somehow. Although the fighter was prone to explode violently if it exceeded light damage, so the flight suit was more for the off chance that the fighter didn't explode. That was also the reason only the most skilled pilots were allowed to pilot fighters, being able to do quick calculations on the fly and get out of trouble.

Heike didn't know how this little flight suit was able to keep someone alive. The FSSA was created to be form fitting. Not that she was embarrassed by it, unlike some other people she knew. As long as the thing did its job and kept her alive, she could live with it. That being said, for both males and females, it could feel very revealing. The suit was made to function like an extra set of armor between the pilot and the environment, or lack of. This necessitated the complete suit to skin contact. At least the was Heike was told.

All of that contact collected real time data, everything from heartrate to hormone balance, and helped balance things out for the pilot. That was what she came up with. Only those brainiacs in the bureau understood it. Heike continued to stare at the disk. She would have it on by now... The way it worked was still confusing even after wearing it countless times.

"Do you want help into the FSSA, Captain?" Fiorenza took off Heike's headphones and reached for the disk. Heike moved her arm away to keep the disk from Fio's reach, then reluctantly handed it to the other girl.

"I guess it wouldn't hurt. I won't get stuck again this time." Heike replied, spreading her arms out.

"That's why the other pilots said to place the apparatus in the middle of your back." Fiorenza explained. "It has to wrap around before it can cover everything."

"I know, but it's still confusing!" Heike snapped. Fiorenza lifted Heike's arms a little higher before pressing the FSSA against her back. Then the suit began to emerge from the disk-like apparatus. The tingling sensation wrapped around her before tightening to force out any excess air. Heike set her headphones on her ears and proceeded to do a couple of kicks and jabs. Satisfied with her movements, she shouted.

"Alright, let's go blow the Vekros into the next system!"

Heike went through the preflight checklist. The engines, life support and such were ready to go, with the exception of the targeting system diagnostics. The other three lautered around her craft until the five-minute warning sounded. It was the normal routine established by them since the other pilots were so full of themselves. Unlike them, Heike was actually a great pilot if she said so herself. She didn't care that she was made for this purpose. It just gave her a better edge than they had.

"Who won the contest last time?" Olivier asked as he poked around the nose-mounted autocannon.

"I think it's pretty obvious. Remember the captain wiped the floor with us. Seriously, who shoots down twenty-three spacecraft in one battle?" Edward answered from the rear of the Barracuda.

"Don't forget you were the one who lost last time either and you still owe all of us." Fiorenza added.

"Oh man! I was hoping you guys forgot that last part." Olivier complained, pulling himself out from under the F-3.

"Hold on! Hotshot pilot coming over here." Fiorenza warned, prompting the other two to join her and Heike by near the cockpit. Heike focused on the data pad with diagnostics.

"This isn't playtime. Why aren't you three standing by at your spacecraft?" The pilot demanded. That set Heike off on the inside.

"The same reason a nobody should mind their own business." Heike threatened, tossing the touchpad onto a toolbox and getting into the face of the pilot.

"It is my damn business you stupid weapon." The pilot tried to reply calmly, though failing to do so. This brought Heike a little satisfaction. "I'm the commanding officer of this wing and ace, Rahsaan Blake."

"Ooohhh, are you now? Never heard of you." Heike crossed her arms. "You look like some newbie. You got to be the same age as us. Temper down that ego, nobody."

"I am, and a hell of a better pilot than you four sorry excuses for ultimate killing machines. Fanged Demon. Paladin. Silent Rain." Rahsaan glared at them, then settled on Heike.

"Then their nonfunctional 'captain', the Adler."

"That's not my- " Rahsaan swiped the side of Heike's head before she could finish, knocking the headphones off. Heike took a couple steps forward to pummel the guy. It took both Edward and Olivier to hold her back while Fio got in between her and the stupid pilot.

"Let me kill him! He deserves it! No one's going to miss him! Let go!" Heike screamed, trying to break free to get the backpedaling pilot.

"See, all you know is how to kill. Do your jobs you dumb guns." Rahsaan taunted by sticking up a middle finger, laughing as he walked away. The five-minute warning sounded, and Heike shouldered out of the other two's loosened grips.

"It would be a shame if he got shot down by enemy fire." Heike murmured as she kicked over the toolbox. Fio picked up on what she said.

"Hey, Lance said to behave remember. We have to get along with the regs." Fiorenza put a hand on Heike's shoulder. Heike only grunted in response, picking up her headphones and resetting them in their original position. All she wanted to do was put that man in his place. Was that too much to ask for?

Heike climbed into the Barracuda and leaned back in the seat. The FSSA connected to the seat with a metallic click, triggering the preflight sequence. Doing a once over of all the dials, the canopy came down with the helmet and shrouded her in darkness. After a few seconds, she was blinded by the heads-up display. An automated voice told them to touch off.

The engines roared as the Barracuda pushed itself off the ground. All the other spacecraft around Heike's did the same, the space between each craft mere inches. The large hangar doors slid open to receive the hovering fighters. Fenrir squad was ahead of the rest and moved to the next set of doors. The entrance into the hangar closed once all of the fighters had entered the chamber, the other doors started to open almost immediately. The spacecraft were propelled out of the chamber with the escaping air.

The engine roar that was so loud before was virtually nonexistent. A dull hum was its replacement. The fighters got into formation as the bombers launched from the carriers. A large chunk of the fleet's destroyer and cruiser escort splintered off in one direction, parallel to the enemy fleet's formation. The Moskva's fighter wing began to creep forward, with the bombers and their carrier-based fighter escort gaining according to Heike's HUD. Three massive vessels awaited them, and they beckoned to her.

"This is Orange Leader; all squads report it." Came the voice of the pilot, she so regretted not slugging in the face. A broken nose would do him some good. One by one, everyone reported in from the Moskva's wing. **"Fenrir squad, report in."**

"Tauchender Adler, ready." Heike grumbled.

"Paladin, ready!"

"Fanged Demon, ready!"

"Silent Rain, all systems are green."

"All squads, protect the bombers so they can cripple the engines of those battleships. I will not tolerate any bombers

being taken out." Blake ordered. Heike could see specks start to grow larger and larger. The HUD began to fill with red markers that represented enemies. She tightened her grip on the yoke. Her chest started to feel constricted, heart pounding in her eardrums, and finally, all thought vanished from her mind as her finger drew closer to the trigger.

5... 4... 3... 2... 1...

Before anything started firing, spacecraft started taking evasive maneuvers. Barracudas and Zeroes went in all directions. Some exploded into metal fragments. A cacophony of voices filled Heike's head as pilots tried to coordinate their defense or were pleading for assistance. The bombers let loose their weapons of any of the Zeroes strayed too close.

Heike fell in behind one Zero and pumped a few rounds into the unsuspecting enemy. She began searching for her next victim as the enemy craft was ripped apart. A Zero zipped by right in front of her, and she turned her Barracuda and tailed the enemy craft. This one knew she was there and began to move erratically.

The targeting sensor would switch from blue to green to blue as the Zero evaded. She was closing the distance and would soon be close enough where it would be impossible to miss. The Zero's speed suddenly increased as another Zero trailed by a Barracuda got in between them. Heike performed a roll to her left to reacquire the target. She fired a couple rounds as the Zero was in midturn, probably to engage her. It didn't matter anymore, as metal fragments burst from the former Zero.

The targeting alert blared as a missile had locked on and launched at her Barracuda. Heike engaged the antilock-on system, and the missile was tricked into hitting that. Whatever had fired that missile was no longer tailing her. *If you want to fight dirty, I can fight dirty too!*

A flip of a switch turned on her lock-on indicator. Finding a suitable target, the indicator began to beep and flash. The beep slowly turned into a constant sound. She let loose a missile and watched it streak towards a Zero. The Zero tried to confuse the missile into hitting something else, but it was too late. The missile impacted just behind the center of the fuselage and the Zero detonated. Another enemy was down.

A painted Zero began to chase her down. It looked to be an enemy squad leader, and an ace at that. Heike made a hard turn one way. The Vekros pilot matched it exactly. There was a scrap between a few Zeroes and a couple Barracudas. She ducked into the three on two hoping to lose her pursuer, taking out one of the Zeroes in the process and evening the odds. The painted Zero had managed to keep track and was still behind her. Pulling the yoke back, the Barracuda began to "climb." The Zero followed her exact pathing.

Pulling it back a little more, she now looked up, or rather down at the battle. The bombers remained untouched, except for one that started to trail after taking a hit. Then she saw the enemy fighter that was just beginning the same maneuver she had just done. It was going to perform it in time. Heike made a b-line towards the Zero and raked it with autocannon fire. The Zero crumpled in on itself.

A friendly fighter nearby was struggling to disengage from an enemy. The stabilizing fin had taken damage which didn't allow the pilot to make crazy maneuvers. She was approaching the friendly head on, so she tilted her wings from one side to another. The other Barracuda copied the movement. Just as it seemed the two would collide, the friendly turned hard enough to get out of the way, but not enough to tear the fighter apart. Heike fired the instant that turn was made and the Vekros craft disappeared. That pilot should be able to make back to their home ship safely.

Now Heike pushed her Barracuda towards the trailing bomber that was starting to get swarmed. She picked out multiple targets for lock-on. Four missiles launched and went to their targets. Three of the Zeroes were taken out. The fourth successfully stopped the missile, but Heike was already upon it. Firing the autocannon, the Zero shuddered and blew into scrap metal.

Whatever was wrong with the Blastray must have gotten fixed as it began to regain speed. Heike took this moment to take stock of her Barracuda's systems. She was completely out of missiles and her autocannon was sitting at fifty percent. The antilock-on system was practically full. The fuel could be better but was still acceptable considering the stunts she pulled.

Heike finally drew the attention of the enemy. Multiple warning indicators popped up. At least four or five Zeroes had dropped everything to pursue her. It would be difficult for all of them to get a shot. Some would be sweating bullets with a five on one, but not Heike. She was starting to get the feeling that her mind was slipping away. Fighting against it, she started pulling hard maneuvers to evade the fire from the Zeroes.

The Zeroes began circling around and attacking from different angles. Performing perfectly timed turns and rolls, none of them hit. She started to counterattack, shooting one and watching the one behind that crash into the remnants of the first. A sharp turn and pushing the Barracuda "down" led to her scoring another kill.

Downing three Zeroes should have made things easier. Those kills she scored were only replaced by three more Vekros fighters. Fuel was going to be a concern if things kept up like this. Pressing a few buttons widened her view. These Vekros sure were trying to pull her number. It wasn't just the five, there had to be at least another eight waiting to join the dogfight.

Then all at once the Zeroes came at her. Autocannon fire came in from multiple directions at once. Pushing the Barracuda as hard as it could go, it leapt through the hail of shells. Heike retaliated with sprays from her autocannon. Two more Zeroes were taken out.

Heike's Barracuda shuddered as it took a hit. A warning indicator popped up reporting to her of the damage sustained. It wasn't that hard to find since a good portion of the battle wasn't on the feed anymore. Otherwise, nothing was about to explode, yet. With four more Zeroes to destroy, Heike put some more juice into the thrusters. It would be a lot more fun to take them all out now, but anymore hits could really ruin her day. Speed and maneuverability were going to be key. Though those two don't really pair, so it was a balancing act between the two.

The dull sound of the engines became a low whine. She needed to split the fighters up and focus on one. Then something came to mind that might work. The Barracuda's nose went "up" as she pushed it towards the ever expansive black. The four Vekros stayed in pursuit. Everything was going according to plan. The Barracuda picked up speed. Warning indicators stated that Heike was straying too far away from the planet's effective gravity pull. *Almost there! Not yet! Not yet! Now!*

Heike cut the engines and pulled a one-eighty. As soon as the Barracuda turned, she punched the engines to full power. The four Zeroes flew past her, probably only realizing what game she was playing. The warnings subsided as Heike started moving in the right direction. Looking back triumphantly, she expected to see the four fighters flailing outside the effective gravity zone. Instead, three of the four fighters were catching up to her. Heike punched the HUD in a fit of rage. *One! All that work for one measly fighter! They aren't even that good! How the hell are they able to keep up?!*

Then Heike remembered something Lance said. *You can't expect the enemy to make mistakes the way you think they will.* For him being younger, he sure had a lot of battle wisdom. Well, it would have been a lot easier if those three Vekros pilots did make the mistake like she wanted. Then an indicator popped up warning the pilot is experiencing too much mental strain.

"Oh, shut up, stupid!" Heike punched the HUD again and the indicator disappeared. She could still keep her bloodlust under control. This was nothing compared to the first time she hopped into one of these. It would still be a lot better if she didn't have to deal with these three bugs. Heike braced for the hits.

"Sorry Captain, we're here to assist." Came the voice of Edward. Watching the screen, three Barracudas ripped into the Zeroes. Heike pulled back to allow the other three to catch up.

"**Nice work Fenrir.**" Heike complimented.

"**Wow! A rare compliment from the Captain herself. What an honor!**" Edward replied jokingly.

"**Hey Captain! Can you throw in a thank you for saving your skin?**" Olivier threw in.

"**Not on your life.**" Heike said flatly.

"**Awww, please. You said we worked really hard.**" Olivier kept begging. He sounded a lot like that idiot, Misha.

"**Are you looking to die?**" Heike snapped.

"**Captain, you know they do this because they know it bothers you.**" Fiorenza reminded.

"**Hmph! They should be glad I even let them.**" Was all Heike said in reply. Edward and Olivier kept trying to get on her bad side.

"**Fenrir! Get back in formation! We're making a run on the middle battleship.**" Orange leader barked. The squad of four caught up quickly. Heike made her way to the front of the pack, while she did this, it gave her time to see how they faired. Most of the EEN fighters were still flying and none of the bombers were lost. The other two bomber formations looked to be in a similar state. Meanwhile, the initial screen of Vekros fighter craft could no longer be considered much of a threat.

The formations of fighters and bombers kept together tightly even in the face of the point defense cannons on the Minotaur battleship. Their best bet would be to dump their load and run like hell. No need to stick around and get shredded by those cannons. The Blastrays were more than capable of crippling the battleship on their first run. Then it was just a matter of assisting in neutralizing the enemy carrier.

The closer they got to the battleship, the more on edge Heike felt. It wasn't herself that thought that way. In fact, she was rather confident that they would win. Something else was causing it, a gut feeling. The sensation of the hairs of her neck sticking straight up. Then she caught it. It was hardly noticeable, but in just the right angle and light. An orange glimmer across the hull of the battleship. She fired a few rounds. *The hell?!*

"Abort the run! Abort the run!" Heike called over the comms. The responses of acknowledgment came through. **"We're just going to hang out for a moment."**

"I didn't say you could give that order gun!" Rahsaan lashed out.

"We can't hit it. Something is there preventing us from doing that." Heike informed and her three subordinates confirmed it.

"That's just the armor. The bombs can punch through that. I'm going to give the order again." Rahsaan said.

"No way meathead. I'm taking charge now." Heike smiled. **"I'm invoking Article 67, beat that you stupid pilot."**

"You can't do that. That has no effect here!" Rahsaan challenged.

"Actually sir, it does. I trust the operator's judgment. I'm not risking my bombers when we don't know what's going on." Came the support of the bombers' commander. Orange Leader cursed at Heike, but she ignored him. She couldn't stop smiling from taking control away from him.

That still left the problem poised in front of her. How could there be something they could hardly see be able to reflect an attack? Maybe the Commander would have a better idea on how to tackle this. Before Heike could get the word out, the battleship opened fire in the direction of the Moskva.

The general quarters alert sounded as the fleet jumped into the Kanto system. The countdown to the battle was now ticking. It would be a stretch if Lera said she was confident, but everything was going to work out. Look what happened on Verdant Prime. Not that it was actually calming her nerves or anything.

A familiar presence walked onto the bridge. She thought of looking for support, but Lera had to focus. This was something she was capable of handling on her own. As his commander, she might just have to put on a show for him. It wasn't every day that she could make an impression like this.

"Alright Commander, all preparations have been made. From this point on, you are the captain of this ship." James clasped a hand on her shoulder before taking a seat. As the bridge crew was updating her on the systems, Lera felt like she wanted to power down. To just go back to her room for a while longer. She stood there awkwardly, swaying one way, glancing nervously at the viewport. Her foot kept up a steady tap against the floor.

"Commander, relax your shoulders. Take a deep breath." Lera did just as Captain James said. After a few breaths she felt a little better.

"Thank you, sir." Lera stood a little taller. "That helped out quite a bit."

"Don't mention it. I just saved you a life of carrying around a single cigar." Blake joked while Lera laughed. Good. She was getting more comfortable by the minute. The reports steadily came in from the other ships saying they were awaiting orders.

"Start the operation!" Lera ordered. The fighters and bombers started leaving the bellies of the Moskva and the carriers. Time for the next movement. "Group Alpha, pull those cruisers and destroyers away from the enemy battleships."

"We are a go." The voice of Alpha's commander said to his ships. Alpha group split off from the main fleet and started its way to where it would threaten the flank of the Vekros fleet. The Vekros response was almost immediate with their cruisers and destroyers moving to intercept. Just as she had planned. The faces of the captains from the other ships looked pleased. The Vekros battleships began to creep forward towards Fifth fleet's carriers that were belonging to the First Assault Group, the EENS Ranger, EENS Eagle, and EENS Jade. They won't have to worry, by the time the enemy battleships were never going to get into firing range. Lera kept an eye on both Alpha and the Vekros battleships while watching the plan view of the battlefield. All the indicators that were moving had congealed into different masses. She zoomed in on specific parts of the screen to get more insight on the battle.

"Commander. The strike group has made contact with enemy interceptors." A sensor tech waved to get her attention.

"Semmelweis, plot course to intercept the enemy carrier." Auri nodded as her fingers glided across the screen. With the course plotted, the Moskva was now playing its part in the battle. Her attention was drawn back to Alpha group. Some of the ships were reporting ineffective enemy fire. Vekros cruisers had slightly better range than the Reno-class cruisers, so she wasn't surprised. Both sides were at their extreme edge of firing range for the main batteries. Lera had ordered the other captains to not fire until the enemy salvos got really uncomfortable. There was no need to waste ammunition and never hit anything.

The same could be said for the Moskva. She was fast by capital ships standards, but it would be another five minutes before any doubts about accurate salvos would be swept aside. The carrier was so far back compared to the rest of the Vekros fleet that even with the railgun, they were more likely to miss. One of the many problems with firing superheavy rounds at near lightspeed was inaccuracy. The further the target, the harder the shot. All the carrier would have to do is a slight course adjustment, which would still be cutting it close, but it has happened. Not to mention running the risk of friendly fire, though such worries weren't present right now.

A steady stream of chatter kept her busy. Lera kept an ear out for the bomber strike group. They had hit resistance and she had already accounted for that. Losses were unfortunately going to occur, but that group's mission was straightforward. The EEN cruisers and destroyers were finally getting hits and receiving some themselves. She micromanaged as much as she could, having ships make minor course adjustments to have a better support net, coordinating fire between multiple ships to take out the more troublesome Vekros ships. Moskva was in range to support Alpha…

"CIC, get a lock on the middle-most cruiser before it takes out the Javelin!" The railgun swiveled to port and took aim. It began to glow blue. "Fire!"

A superheavy round leapt out of rails at a speed Lera couldn't keep up with. A small blue light impacted the cruiser followed by an explosion. The Vekros cruiser wasn't destroyed, but the light of its engines went out. It was effectively dead in the water as the saying went. The EENS Javelin replied with gratitude, firing a sweep of torpedoes at the helpless enemy.

"Commander, the enemy carrier is now in effective firing range."

"CIC, switch target to the carrier." Lera couldn't get the second order out when the alarms started blaring.

"Enemy battleships firing!" The tech shouted. Lera looked over just as the three Minotaur's fired a salvo each. The computer had the trajectory going right by the Moskva. Were they shooting at them, or…

"Hold the course! If we stray, then we get hit!" All the crew on the bridge braced against their consoles. The shells just barely passed the top of the hull between the bridge and the railgun, close enough that some paint might have been scratched off. Lera followed their path and watched them impact an EEN vessel. It blew up in a spectacular fashion. There weren't going to be any survivors from that ship.

"We just lost contact from the cruiser, EENS Taranto." The sensor tech said begrudgingly. Everything was going so smoothly and just like that, nearly seven and a half thousand lives were taken into the void. Lera was just about to connect with Orange Leader and noticed, to her surprise, that Heike had taken over command. It had to be for a good reason, she hoped.

"Adler! Talk to me!" Lera opened up a one-on-one channel with Fenrir's captain.

"I can't explain it commander. There's this shiny orange layer, but I can't see it normally." Heike was talking so fast that Lera could hardly understand what she was trying to say. Heike was in an intense, high adrenaline fight after all.

"Hey! Slow down. Orange what?"

"Our attacks! They won't land. They just sort of reflect." Heike replied with slight agitation.

"What do you mean?" Lera pressed for more information.

"Hell, I don't know! They just reflect, not like a ricochet." There was a long pause before Heike shouted. **"That orange glow has to be the cause! It's the only thing I can think of."**

"Got it. Hold your position until I have further orders." Lera also gave the order for Alpha to press the attack. It was better to keep them going and possibly get a victory through their efforts. What Heike said didn't make a whole lot of sense. Why was she talking about an orange glow? The system's star gave off an orange color, but that didn't have any relevance here. Whatever it was, Lera had to come up with a countermeasure fast. If only Heike's description could be better. If it was Vekros related, then what kind of technology could reflect attacks? Why do the battleships have them and not the cruisers or destroyers?

"Is CIC locked on to the carrier?" Lera asked and was met by a thumbs up. "Fire!"

The railgun glowed blue and fired. The shell tracked right towards the carrier. Then it miraculously changed trajectory when it should have hit the carrier. The officer reported a negative impact. Lera frowned more out of frustration than surprise. If the battleships couldn't be hit, then it was obviously the same with their carrier. Both types of ships had the same technology preventing them from harm; there was only one idea she had about what it could be, and it sounded too tacky for her. It had to be a shield, or a field generator of some kind. She was basing it off a show she watched, but who knew its applications would actually be spot on in these circumstances.

Lera had identified the problem, that still didn't tell her how to circumvent it. She needed to find a solution before any more damage could be down to the fleet, ships were expensive, but the crews even more so. How does it work? What is powering the field? These were questions not to be solving during combat, rather a longer process that was too late to implement now. Of all the times to encounter something like this. Another explosion rattled her concentration as they lost the destroyer EENS Jaguar. The two destroyers EENS Nicholas and Umikaze were heavily damaged from the other's destruction and stray rounds.

This might not be the wrong assumption, but since the shield was around the hull, it wouldn't be wrong to assume the shield was powered through the ship itself. There was a slight probability that it was coming from the planet and there would be plenty of energy to do that. The problem with that was that there would be a delay, and any hits would cause the shield to dissipate. How long was something she didn't know but it didn't matter here. Every ship was powered by Aurelet crystals, and those crystals could power almost anything. They were so versatile that as long as they were properly contained, theoretically, they could be used as a catalyst to produce a reflective field. This was more up Oskar's alley than hers, so she was just guessing.

"Scan the carrier. Search for spots where the power is strained." If she was right about this, then there was a definite way to beat them. The techs got to work as they watched the screen for any signs. It took a few scans before anything of interest was revealed. The reactors weren't under any strain themselves, but an irregular electrical junction within the ship near the bridge was showing to be working under strenuous conditions.

In the history of anything electronic, the best way to take it out was through electromagnetic pulse, or EMP weapons. The bad news was that no such weapon, at least right now, had the power to knock out a robust grid network the Vekros used, let alone ones on a battleship. There was one other way, but Lera loathed the idea of having to use them. These were always used as a last resort. They wouldn't need to use them if technology was able to keep up with the demands of this war.

"Captain James? Do we have any nukes aboard the Moskva?" Lera looked back at the man sitting comfortably in the captain's chair. Despite the situation, he looked rather calm.

"Yes. Except they aren't loaded into their launchers. We weren't expecting to be bombing any planets." The captain replied. If that were the case, then it would require a huge team to get those loaded. She might have to call one of the carriers to have a spacecraft specially equipped with one to take out the shields. That would run the risk of having it shot up and destroying them instead.

"Commander! I'll get it loaded, just keep things going up here and I'll let you know when they're in." Lance rushed out of the bridge before Lera could get a word off. She had no idea if he had any clue on how to load them, but if Lance said that he could do it, then she wouldn't doubt him.

"Must be nice to be such an eager soldier." The captain smiled. Lera didn't understand what Blake meant by that, unless he was reminiscing, but for now she had to focus on not losing any more ships. She had to trust that Lance was going to do what he always does.

Lance knew he was getting involved in the operation rather early. This battle was supposed to be a small break for him. It also didn't take a tactical genius to see that the fleet was in a rough spot currently. Hence, why he didn't want to stand by and let Kurepina handle everything. The Moskva's crew could handle the arming of the nuclear weapons, but he was tired of being idle. If it helped the commander, then it was worth doing.

"Williams? Gunnery Chief, do you copy?" Lance talked into the earpiece as he hit the elevator button.

"This is Williams." Came her reply.

"This is Revenant. Can you spare a crew to the starboard side launch room?" Lance rushed out of the elevator to that area.

"Howdy Revenant! Give me a moment and I'll bring some guys over." After she finished, Lance switched his target of communication to Ryder.

"Ryder! Bring A'Darrion, Rene, Lek, and Misha over to the starboard launch room."

"Sure thing, boss." Ryder grinned through the earpiece. Good. Between the gunnery chief's crew and Lance's team, it should be more than enough to do the prep work. They knew the fundamentals of nuclear weaponry and how to survive nuclear fallout. It was something they learned at Athena. From now, all the way back to the earliest of human conflicts on Earth. All the strategies and tactics, weaponry and technology, it was all drilled into them.

The space he entered was massive. This launch room spanned three decks up. Lance could tell that the crew that was stationed here left in a hurry with the large mess that was left behind. Towards the back of the space where he was were four large missiles. Perhaps eighteen meters in length set on tracks. If they were planet side, those would be Intercontinental Ballistic Missiles, or ICBMs. Turns out they were effective from space as well, with a hell of a lot more destruction.

The sound of many footsteps running grabbed his attention from the space. He was greeted with the sight of Ryder and Ashley Williams teams. Lance knew it was rather urgent for them to get here as quickly as possible, but he wasn't expecting them to show up this quickly. He wasn't going to complain, it just meant they were going to win faster.

"You guys showed up rather quickly." Lance greeted the two groups as they began to split off.

"You know, just got tired of not being included in any of the action." Ryder smiled.

"I couldn't let you guys play with these puppies without my supervision. They're my special toys after all." Williams pointed at the four nuclear missiles. "We at least don't have to worry about targeting. That is something the commander is in control of."

Two of the missiles started to slide across the tracks towards the launch tubes. The other two moved momentarily before their progress was halted. A group of technicians gathered around a console. The commotion caught the attention of the gunnery chief.

"What's the problem? Get the other two nukes loaded already!" Williams stomped over to the group.

"There's a problem, the carts aren't responding to the command. There might be a fault in the code." The lead technician informed.

"Can we fix it?" Williams queried as she looked over the information displayed on the screen.

"Unfortunately, we would need the shipwright master code, so no. We'll have to wait until we are back at Yire." The technician replied flatly.

"Of all the times to have a malfunction…" Williams put two fingers to the bridge of her nose. "Fine. We'll have to manually move the carts. They should raise on their own once we get them under the launch tubes."

"Let my guys handle this. Get everything else ready." Williams replied with a thumbs up before barking orders at her men. Lance rushed over to where Ryder and the other three had gathered after finishing their tasks.

"Alright. Ready for a strength test?" Lance pointed in the direction of the two missiles.

"You're joking." Rene stared at the nukes.

"There's two. You know what that means A'Darrion?" Ryder looked over at the other guy who had the same competitive look.

"Whoever gets their missile to the finish last has to do deadlifts until the other says to stop." A'Darrion challenged.

"Deal!" The two musclemen bumped fists. Lek came over to join them after helping with the techs.

"Rene and Ryder, you're with me. A'Darrion, Misha, and Lek, handle the other one." The two teams went to their respective missiles. Ryder and A'Darrion made it clear they wanted the closest ends to each other. "On three. One. Two. Three!"

The two teams started pushing the carts, grunting with effort. It felt like the carts moved by the inches at a time. Ryder and A'Darrion were spurring the others on. Even with their enhanced physical strength, this was still a lot harder than the operators made it look. A couple of them slipped a little trying to get traction to push the heavy weaponry forward. The regs would have had a worse time trying to get these missiles to move. Lance felt like his knees were standing in fire. Then the cart suddenly stopped, and the missile began to rise.

"Let's go!" Rene tugged on Lance's arm. The two teams vacated to a safer area. Now it was all up to Kurepina. *All right Commander, I did my part. Finish them off!*

Lera knew that it would take some time, but she didn't know how much her patience could hold. She wasn't very much enjoying this. They haven't lost any more ships thanks to her efforts. When the Minotaurs fired, the techs would trace the projectile path to the targeted ships, and she gave a course correction to that vessel accordingly. This could only keep going for so long before she or the other ships' captains slipped up. Some ships still had taken some hits and were losing power.

The spacecraft from the carriers were starting to thin out too. The Vekros battleships' point defense was just too potent. At this point, it would be better for them to withdraw and rearm. Then that would leave Alpha group to receive the undivided attention of the enemy battleships. They would be caught in a worse crossfire from the Vekros cruisers and battleships. Those fighter groups were definitely providing a good distraction.

"Gunnery Chief Williams here. We ran into some trouble. We have a workaround but give us a few more minutes." Lera wasn't expecting to hear Ashley's voice. Hopefully whatever issue she was talking about was minor, but she herself had to prepare for when the nukes were ready.

"Arizona. Kongo. Have your guns ready to fire on the enemy battleships. Howe and Nevada, move up into the firing line and be prepared to fire as well. Adler, nukes are going to be inbound. I trust you know the blast radius."

All groups carried out their orders accordingly. She made sure CIC still had a lock on the carrier. There was no way of knowing if the shields would be out temporarily or permanently, so she erred on the side of caution. The Moskva was close enough to use the railgun and the six main battery guns to fire. It all came down to whether the nukes would interfere with the Vekros' systems.

"Ready to launch!" Not a second after those words were uttered, Lera pressed the button. Four hatches opened on the starboard side followed by four missiles leaving the ship. The four tracks were plotted on a screen in front of her. One by one, the missiles impacted their targets. Each blast brought with it a brilliant light that Lera had to shield her eyes from.

Then the crew on the bridge began to cheer. Lera looked at the latest scans just as the blasts subsided. There may be interference from the radiation, but scans did show that the Vekros' power systems had overloaded. Those Minotaurs were now sitting ducks. The four friendly battleships fired a salvo as the spacecraft went around to start their attack run. With that, Lera turned back towards the Aries-class carrier.

The onboard systems were all reporting alerts and the HUD blinked out a few times. Eventually the view was restored. The commander's gambit worked, the targets were now drifting, and fires had sprouted up from their interior. She usually was a fan of all this high maneuvering, but sights like this where victory was close at hand couldn't be passed up. It also gave her some inspiration.

"Let's go Silent Rain!" Her captain shouted. Fiorenza kicked her Barracuda into high gear. Some point defense cannons were still operable, their fire was no longer effective. The mass of fighters that swarmed them earlier had also been annihilated. A few dozen Vekros Zeros remained. The Blastrays followed closely to the Barracudas, smelling the blood in the water like sharks. She provided cover for the bombers as they bombed the battleships. Seconds after explosions took out the engines for good, superheavy shells tore into the armor of the helpless battleships. Catastrophic damage occurred from the salvos, and the Minotaurs began to break apart as they were rocked by explosions.

The Barracuda that contained Orange Leader strayed to close to the exploding battleships and took a hit from debris. The Barracuda spun out of control away from everyone else. It didn't look like anyone noticed that the former lead's blip had blinked out from the rest. Fio started turning her Barracuda around to go after the other.

"Keep going Fio. I'll go save his ass." Heike ordered.

"Are you sure?"

"Yeah. I'd rather see him safe than be reprimanded by those two for letting him burn up in the atmosphere." Fio pressed a small signal button that stood for acknowledged.

Fiorenza and the spacecraft turned toward the enemy cruisers and destroyers that were a good way away. This gave her a full view of the Moskva as it fired all of its main weapons. The railgun hit first, and the carrier detonated instantly. Then six superheavy shells slammed into the burning husk for good measure. Whatever Vekros were left didn't stand a chance, it was clear victory. Fio was going to remember that sight of the Moskva's awe-inspiring firepower for a long time.

The crew went around congratulating each other. Cheering, hugs, and handshakes went around the room. Captain James came behind Lera and patted her on the shoulder. It was time for her to tap out and let the captain handle the stragglers. This was the Moskva's second major victory among the numerous smaller ones. Watching the crew celebrate made her happy, it was the kind of thing all leaders wanted to see. Lera stuck around on the bridge for the battle's completion. It didn't take longer than ten minutes. Without leadership, the leftover Vekros couldn't mount a coherent front and were utterly decimated by the firepower of the EEN.

The Moskva's fighter wing was returning from their sortie. Lera was going to meet them as they landed, then she realized they would want to enjoy the victory by themselves first. She made some post battle rounds to other decks before waiting at the locker area where Fenrir was. She wanted to be the first to congratulate them before the other two squads could. From what she heard; they had a really high kill count between the four of them. Lera didn't understand the quest for kills as a pilot, tank ace, and other units; she was just glad Fenrir returned unharmed. Heike was the first one out followed by her squad mates.

"You should use those more often!" Heike exclaimed. "It's so much better not being shot at."

"Well, we can't. The governments on Earth frown upon the use of nuclear weapons and see them as a last resort. Plus, they have gotten rather expensive to manufacture anymore. If that isn't enough, I don't like using them either." Lera explained.

"Boo, that's no fun." Heike pouted while kicking at the floor.

"Anyway, you guys did an amazing job. Keep up the good work and Fenrir might win squad of the year. Yeah, I heard about you operators' little competition." Lera enticed. Heike beamed with pride as the others gave each other high fives.

"Going off of that, looks like Captain won again this time. Even after saving Orange Leader." Edward mumbled the last part "I got dead last."

"Heike? You saved Orange Leader?" Lera asked.

"Yeah, she did! Go on, tell her Cap!" Olivier encouraged.

"Don't wanna." Heike refused as she shot him a look.

"Fine, I will." Olivier began his retelling. "So, the Cap turned off and followed the spinning Barracuda. Mind you that it was hurtling towards the planet and a very high speed. The Captain has to line up both fighters perfectly so she can engage a cable link between them. Somehow, she does this, strongarms her way to the other side, opens the canopy and strongarms her way back with the other guy's unconscious body. I'm surprised that she did that after what he did to her earlier."

Heike elbowed Olivier in the gut, leaving him half-bent over in pain. It was too late. Lera, who was enjoying the story, narrowed her eyes at them. She took a step towards Olivier and brought him back up.

"What did he do?" Lera demanded.

"Nothing Commander. It was- "Lera put up a hand to stop Heike from saying anything else. Whether she was hiding it for her pride or something else, Lera wasn't going to let her.

"Well. Uhm, you see, he may or may not have called us weapons, aaaand he possibly wacked the captain across the side of her head." Olivier stammered. Lera stepped away. *Seriously, after I went over this with the crew the first time around. Not to mention how long they have been working together now!*

Lera stormed off to the infirmary. The voice of Heike complaining that Lance was going to kill followed. Well, that meant Lera had to protect Heike from whatever she thought Lance was going to do too. It didn't take her long to reach the medical wing. Rahsaan Blake, Orange Leader, sat up in his bed when she entered his room.

"To what do I owe this pleasure, Commander?" Rahsaan asked blissfully unaware of his wrongdoing. That made Lera even angrier.

"Quiet! I heard what you did to Heike and Fenrir today. What makes you think you have any right to do that!?" Lera was struggling to keep herself from yelling. Others were around trying to get better from their wounds, and it would be rude to interrupt that. Yet it was still unbelievably hard to contain her anger.

"It's my right. I did nothing wrong; they aren't even people after all. That bitch deserved it anyhow, getting up in my face like that. She's lucky she's not a se- "Lera couldn't listen to this.

"Shut your mouth right now." Lera interrupted.

"Why? Why does it matter what I did?" Rahsaan glared at her.

"It is wrong! How many times must I explain this! Don't believe the words you are told. What do your eyes see? Do the operators look like robots? Androids? Nothing to say, right? At this point the operators are more human than we are. How can you treat your fellow man like this? Does your conscience not tell you that it's wrong?"

Rahsaan refused to look at her. Instead, he stared at the corner of the room. Lera was beyond angry at this beyond. She gripped her crossed arms so hard that the blood flow may have stopped. She turned on her heel to walk out.

"We're going to review footage and comms from today. You'll be suspended and demoted according to the level we deem fit. Also, you'll be transferred to another unit. Don't even try to fight it, it's practically a done deal."

Lera left the pilot with his thoughts. She let out a breath, that felt a little better to get that off of her chest, but now she was just frustrated. How many times had she explained herself now? How many times did she need to explain the operators' plight? Probably more than she can count by now. Even if she had to do it a hundred, no, a million times, she'd always be on the side of the operators. She'll always be on his side.

She said to never give up... I fear he is truly lost.

Rene Carey, Journal

Chapter 3

Flak

"This isn't going to work." Lance grumbled at the commander. She held out the bottle for him to read. He spun it around to know what they were getting into.

"Trust me, it will. She'll need this before we go to the surface." Commander Kurepina assured. She flipped around to talk to him while she backstepped. "I worked really hard to procure those too. She's been working hard and has been more cooperative. Honestly, you should give her credit for trying to change. Did something happen between you two before?"

"Not particularly." Lance handed the bottle back to the commander.

"That's such a *you* answer." She bowed her head in disappointment.

"What does that mean?"

"It means that you need to trust that I can convince her." Kurepina looked confident and it showed in her walk. She must be still riding that victory.

"I believe that you could, when Rose sprouts wings. Heike's had an aversion from medicine from… before we became operators." Lance stared off into space as a memory of him and those three in that small room came to mind.

"Just watch me. This will be easier than pushing those nukes around." Lance caught a gleam in her eyes that made him want to believe her. As they made their way down the corridors of the Moskva, he couldn't help but watch Kurepina.

The way she carried herself was unlike anyone he'd ever seen. Her walk was elegant, like in the books of fantasy worlds, yet full of purpose. The commander may not like it, but she really was something of a princess, at least in Lance's eyes. He'd noticed over the past six months when they walked side by side, they were nearly shoulder to shoulder. Sometimes, just enough of her arm would brush against his to where he'd notice. The hint of the scent of flowers that followed her around seemed to flood his mind. For the first time, Lance truly enjoyed the company of another person.

"Huh? Why are you staring at me?" The commander noticed him watching from the corner of her eye and wiped her cheek. "There isn't something on my face, is there?"

"Not at all. I'm just trying to figure out how the princess can get a hold of this stuff." Lance teased.

"Hmmm! I said to not call me that." Kurepina frowned.

"I'll remember that next time." Lance replied amused, like he had any intention of doing that.

"Yeah? You said that last time too. Don't forget it then." Kurepina lightly punched his arm.

They found Heike waiting by the shuttle that would be taking the operators to Kanto-IV's atmosphere. She looked to be making last-minute adjustments to the flight packs they would be using. It was very much unlike her to take responsibility for equipment. Heike was either itching to get into a fight or was ready for a change of scenery. He was still impressed that she even tried to do anything prep related.

"Heike! Come here, please!" the commander called out. Heike looked up and recognized who had called her as she promptly approached them.

"Hi, Commander. I, uhm, want to thank you for what you did earlier." Heike looked away embarrassed, then pointed at Lance. "And I'm not saying this because he told me to!"

Lance should have known she would pull something like this. He held up his hands defensively and shook his head. The commander looked between the two, putting her hands on her hips and bowing her head. Then when she raised it, she was laughing. Lance looked at Heike for any clue as to what was happening, though she gave him no answer.

"I swear, for being the best of humanity, you sure act like a bunch of school kids. Although, it can be cute sometimes." Kurepina cast a glance at Lance who pretended not to notice.

"So, you needed me for something." Heike asked enthusiastically.

"Yeah, here. Take this." Commander Kurepina handed it over to Heike who looked it over suspiciously.

"What the hell is this? I can't read anything on it?" Heike turned to bottle round and round trying to say the name of the medication.

"It's a..." Lance trailed off not sure what to come up with when Lera held a hand up to him.

"It's medication. All you do is mix it in a drink as you take it once a day. It will provide a tremendous boost in energy and will help you with controlling some of your other issues." Heike looked over the bottle again while Lance was thinking that telling her outright was the wrong play.

"Fine. If it helps, it helps." Heike replied understandingly, much to Lance's surprise.

"I thought you avoided medication?" Lance asked, which brought Heike to look at him like he was stupid.

"That's not it. You guys just had that preconception that I didn't like medicine and would lie to me about what it was. I hated that, so I didn't take it on purpose. If you guys treated me like any other person, I would have taken it no problem." Lance couldn't follow that logic, but Heike continued. "I'll give you two a pass. You have been gone for a long time and you're just new. But please, treat me like normally next time."

As Heike walked away, Kurepina shot Lance look that said she was right. He really didn't think it would be that easy to convince Heike, yet they didn't have to try. The other captain just accepted it. Lance had this entire thing planned out to make her take the medication and if he hadn't faltered, he would have been the one that was right. The commander held out a fist, which Lance completed the gesture that was their victory, unsatisfying as it was.

"I told you that you don't give her enough credit." Kurepina reminded.

"Yeah... I guess you're right. This time." Lance admitted defeat. The commander checked the time and looked disappointed.

"I must prepare myself. You guys be careful, especially you, Captain Field. Sorry I wasn't able to keep you from going in solo." Kurepina fretted, her words dripped with anxiety as her head drooped to the floor.

"We'll be fine Commander. Ryder can handle those guys and I'll have Dog with me. Just do what you always do, and all of us will be back here in no time." Lance replied as comforting as he could.

"That's a promise then." Kurepina smiled.

The shuttle interior began to blink green from the lights over the doors with the turbulence subsiding. Everyone always looked so serious on these flights. Each member of the three squads psyching themselves up. It's not to say that Chika wasn't serious about the mission. She had been doing this kind of thing for so long now that it didn't bother her like it used to. It was only when Rene was getting himself into trouble, like on Verdant Prime, that was when reality would affect her. *Heh, that makes me feel more like Heike.*

"Alright operators, be advised, a sizeable Vekros force will be present in your area. Vice-Captain, you are to lead Fenrir, Hellfire, and Cerberus squads to retake the Fort Johnston Complex. There is a long list of tasks that need to be completed before you can advance any further from there. Take out the AA and wipe out all enemy forces on the airfield if you want a resupply. Keep in mind that this will be a drop point for more of our landing forces in the future. Take out all gun emplacements enroute to the enemy command center. This will give us control of the Aargblast region and allow the second set of landings to happen without interference. Once completed, make your way through the towns and clear them out until we rendezvous outside Potzlan."

"Roger that Commander, this will be easy." Ryder replied to the orders.

"Captain Field, as we discussed before, you'll be heading to Marvburg and infiltrate the captured intelligence center. Look out for the building named Raveset. It was a former computer software company before being converted into a combat information center at the onset of the war. No doubt the Vekros have been using it for themselves, so dig up what you can about the enemy forces and get to Potzlan."

"Consider it done." Lance responded distantly. Chika noticed the thousand-mile stare he got right before a mission. She had seen that stare countless times before he became almost superhuman even compared to operator standards.

"I'm counting on you guys. Don't take any unnecessary risks, if you can't complete a mission, there is no shame in not

being able to complete it. Your priority should be coming back alive. We still have to win a war after all."

Though there was no way of telling, Chika swore the commander's presence faded away, leaving them to do what they did best. An unsettling quietness hung in the air. Chika really couldn't believe them right now. After all that talk and confidence they resort to staying in their own thoughts.

"Hey VC, do you have any words of encouragement for us?" Chika suggested. Ryder looked surprised and found a bunch of eyes on him. The vice-captain tapped the top of his LMG with one finger, slow and steady.

"If I had to say- Let's make our commander proud and kick some ass!" Ryder raised his fist into the air while the others shouted in agreement. The assault shuttle deaccelerated until it was at a crawl, the warning lights were no longer blinking. Chika put on the oxygen mask and made sure the glide wings were in good order. The doors opened up to a beautiful starry night.

"Ryder, look out for them for me." Lance expressed before falling backwards out of the shuttle. Chika, Heike, and Rene all stepped to the edge of the side he was on. She could just barely make out his figure gliding away in the darkness. It was time for the rest of them to do the same. She waited for no one and leapt right of the assault shuttle with a thrilled yell. She could feel that Heike was right on her heels with that jump. The glide wings came out automatically after freefalling for a certain distance. Chika had only used these a couple times, but it was just as fun as the last time.

Now they just had to glide for the next twenty minutes to the LZ. The mask displayed their ETA, location, and location of other squad members. Though she wasn't paying attention to that. The starry sky kept her from focusing on anything else. Only hours ago, there was a battle above the planet. From down here, she couldn't tell that's what had happened. Just like she couldn't tell the Vekros were waiting below them. It was just Chika, her friends, and the stars watching over them. These were the kind of moments that made the feeling of fighting for your own survival seem so far away.

Chika reveled at the beauty of the sky all the way through the twenty-minute glide. The landing wasn't soft by any means. Fortunately, with the help of their enhanced physical strength, all they were going to feel was some bruises. It took several minutes to gather together. They landed about a half-mile north of the LZ into a grouping of trees, which nearly caused some of them to get stuck. Other than that small error, the small trek started without a hitch.

It didn't take long to get to where they were headed. Peering through the night vision, Chika could just make out a Vekros patrol. If Vekros suits didn't hide body heat so well, thermal imaging would have allowed her to spot them a lot sooner. Heike and Misha crept closer and closer to the approaching foot soldiers. Heike aimed her two silenced pistols and fired four times, taking out four. Misha used a combat knife to slit the throat of one and threw it into the helmet of the other before it could raise its gun up. If the Vekros weren't already on alert, that gave the squads fifteen more minutes of extra breathing room. If the Vekros did notice, it was going to get interesting really fast.

"Ryder, they took out the patrol. The way should be clear, and we should reach the airfield shortly." Chika informed. Ryder came and knelt next to her to confirm.

"That's great. I'm not liking how open the ground is with little in the way of cover, but we couldn't have just left that patrol alone either. Let's cut through this area ASAP."

"On top of that, suns up in three hours and we still have to clear out roughly four miles worth of enemies." Rene added from behind them. Ryder closed his eyes to think.

"Alright, we'll have to split the job here. Rene, take Lek and A'Darrion and take the far side of the airfield. Fio, Edward, and Olivier, go cause some havoc in the hangers. Chika, you're with me." Ryder handed out orders.

"Heike and Misha, start heading towards the gun emplacements and take them out quietly."

"Where are we going?" Chika asked as she followed Ryder.

"I think we can handle the control tower, maybe the whole damn terminal if you're up to it." Ryder replied, his voice strained with excitement.

"Might as well if we want to get more supplies." Chika motioned to the limited number of magazines they both carried. Leaving the concealment, Chika and Ryder stayed to the edge of one of the runways. From what she could tell, the Vekros had centered around the control tower. It looked like work was being done to convert the structure so that it would be more suited for the Vekros.

Stopping to assess the area further, Chika could just make out the silhouette of a Valence tank underneath a tarp-like object. She pointed out the tank to Ryder who motioned his hand from side to side in reply. A maybe. Instead of moving on to the control tower, he moved toward the tank. When they got in for a closer look, it was clearly guarded by its crew and two additional squads of Vekros foot soldiers. Looking at Ryder, he shook his head. Before the two could move on, an explosion rocked the night air as one of the hangers became an inferno. Bright flames licked the sky as secondary explosions continued to sound off.

Heike fired a round into the helmet of the foot soldier, watching orange flames illuminate the hangers and the control tower. Whoever that was is having a lot more fun than she was at the moment, not to mention being stuck with Misha as her partner. The pair had already disabled two gun emplacements and were now working on the third. She could hear him moving around different parts around the breech of the big gun behind her. After this one, there were five more.

"You take too long to break something." Heike complained. She peeked her head over the ground in the direction of the next target.

"A man's best work is done in silence. But in all seriousness, disabling isn't the same thing as breaking." Misha shuffled on his knees to the other side of the breech.

"Sure it is. Just take a few parts off." Heike leaned against the sheet metal lined wall.

"Right. As soon as you can tell me what a breech block is."

"Shut up! That's a trick question!" Heike pushed herself off the wall to look at the part of the large-caliber weapon he was working around.

"It really isn't and keep your voice down. I don't want to be shot in the back because you can't control your own volume." Misha hissed. Heike kicked where he was about to place his left hand.

"Don't do that!" Heike looked back over at the orange blaze. Then an idea came to her. Stacked neatly in the corner was the ammunition for this weapon, so...

"Hey, did you bring any 'plastics' with you?" Misha's hands stopped working and he gave a sidelong glance.

"Of course I did. What do you have in mind?" Misha asked.

"I just don't want to be out done is all."

The armor-clad enemy moved without a moment's hesitation. Almost all headed in the direction of the burning hanger, weapons at the ready. The two squads that were stationed around the taken also headed that way, only leaving the crew to get the tank ready. Chika could practically hear the smile on Ryder's face as he watched the enemy move away from the tank. Chika raised her rifle and fired rounds in quick succession, picking off the crew that was about to enter the

Valence. Each was a clean shot, without alerting any nearby enemies. As the two reached the tank, she pulled out a grenade.

"Woah, woah, woah. What are you doing?" Ryder pushed her hand away from the firing pin.

"I thought we were going to disable the tank." Chika looked questioningly at the man who was already halfway down the driver's hatch.

"Hell no! I have a better idea." Ryder disappeared into the hatch and called from inside. "Come on and get in already! You can man the turret!"

Chika was already bot liking the idea he had in mind as she climbed down into the tank. When she got off the ladder, she was met the breech of whatever gun this thing was equipped with as well as a bunch of black-out computer screens. Moving a little further into the vehicle, Ryder was getting comfortable in the driver's seat, pressing buttons on the screen at random. Compared to her, his large body looked cramped inside this thing.

"Do you have any idea what that says?" Chika questioned as she went back up to glance at the screen at the commander's seat.

"No, but if I press enough buttons, this thing is bound to unlock." Ryder replied as the edges of the screen turned green. The turn of the ignition and a flip of a switch coupled with the pull of a lever and the engine roared to life. After a few seconds, it turned into a low purr.

"Listen to the sound of that! It works similarly enough to our tanks." Ryder said amazed then looked back at Chika. "Get in the turret and get ready to shoot."

"What? I'm sure the firing systems are locked too." Chika turned back towards him.

"I meant use the machine gun on top of the turret. If you have to, use the coaxial machine gun in the turret." Ryder clarified as the tank began to move.

"No, I'd rather be outside of this metal deathtrap." Chika mumbled, climbing back out of the turret. She checked the machine gun's ammo supply before deciding it was acceptable. Since this was a heavy machine gun, she moved it swiveled back and forth, noting how much heavier it was compared to the LMG that Ryder and A'Darrion carried around, and it was stabilized on a mount at that. The engine was so loud Chika could barely make out the sounds of gunfire from the hangers and the other side of the airfield.

Ahead of her, the Vekros that were around the control tower started to approach the oncoming tank. Their weapons were down from what Chika could tell. Lining the machine gun to the furthest one back, she opened up on the unsuspecting Vekros. They reacted faster than she thought they would have, diving to the ground to make them smaller targets, to throw off her aim, or make her lose sight of them.

Her night vision might be a little off from the blaze in the hanger, but it was enough to still see them clearly. She didn't miss a single target as the prone foot soldiers tried to crawl away or fired potshots. Heavy return fire soon hit the tank as a couple enemy machine guns revealed their location. Ryder must have caught sight of them as the Valence veered right into the hailstorm of bullets. Chika had to duck down into the hatch and wait for the right moment to shoot back.

Chika watched the Vekros continue to fire from the optics in the cupola. The muzzle flashes came from behind worn-down sandbags. By now the crew of those MGs had to know that it was pointless to keep up ineffective fire. The machine guns indeed ceased fire and the crew abandoned the spot. They were at her mercy now. Chika popped back up and fired into the backs of the six fleeing enemies. Bullets started flying in from the direction of the control tower. Returning fire, Chika took out the units that were in front of the control tower's entrance. The tank stopped near the entryway to the building. Grabbing her assault rifle, she happily hopped off the metal deathtrap.

"Do you think you can manage on your own for a bit? I want to go get the other three." The tone from Ryder's voice sounded like he just wanted to play with the giant death mobile more.

"Yeah, go play with your new toy." Chika replied.

"That's not- You got me." He confirmed as he drove away. **"We'll back you as soon as we can."**

It had been a while since Chika had to solo an enemy force. This was a large building that had to have enemies around every corner. As much as it was nice to have backup, sometimes there was pent-up anger and frustration that needed to be released that no other way could satisfy. It was better that the others didn't see her bad side. *Come on out, so I can wipe the floor with you!*

Lance scanned the area outside of the Raveset building. It was heavily guarded from what he could see from up here. Good thing he decided to land on top of the building and clear the hostiles up here first. Trying to sneak through all of those patrols and defensive positions would just take too long. After memorizing the enemy positions and strength, Lance silently lifted open the rooftop access hatch.

There were no immediate threats around the hatch. Lance descended the ladder into the Raveset building. The ladder was above the floor by ten feet, so he leapt to the ground and landed as quietly as a cat. The information center was fifteen floors down from this one. These top floors must not be frequented as much as the area looked hardly disturbed. He decided it was best to check these floors as well. This was a former EEN information hub after all. There could be all manner of lost data here. Going room by room, most of the offices and meeting areas didn't contain useful information. There were some books that seemed interesting, though he didn't have the space to carry them. After going down seven floors, there still was no sign of any enemy presence aside from the roof. Lance was about to skip a room when he saw the name displayed on the door.

Farver.

Lance opened the door slowly. *Was she here before? Why of all places would she have been here? Whatever it was, it might have some clues to...*

When he opened the door, he was surprised at how untouched this room was. The other rooms he had entered had been nothing but a mess. This one looked frozen in time. Almost like a time capsule. Besides all the dust, it was like Farver had never left. Her organization, the way the focal points of the room were set, even the same the exact same coffee mug was in the same position he would see it at Athena.

Lance began his search for the room. For some reason, it felt wrong to disturb the set up. Whatever he picked up, he made sure to place it exactly the way it was before he touched it. The bookshelf contained topics that were way above his understanding. Genetics, biology, DNA transmutation, and other names that got harder and harder to understand the further down he read. The frame that hung on the wall behind the desk contained a degree for something he didn't understand. The picture frame on the desk contained a photo. He recognized two people instantly. It was Farver and the Chief, albeit a lot younger than he knew them. The third person Lance hadn't the faintest idea of who he was. Flipping over the picture, some words were scribbled on the back.

Amante, Adolf, and I

Spring Break, March 29th, 2392

Lance set the picture back down and picked up the file that was sitting on top of the desk. His blood turned to ice as he saw the name on the file. Flashbacks from his time in Athena Corps flooded his head. The unrelentless training, the dark interior, needles and bright lights, blood, screams, and heartless "caretakers". For some odd reason, his hands began to tremble. He fumbled with the page before he was finally able to turn it over. What he saw wasn't what he was quite expecting to see first. It was a letter addressed to Farver.

Adolf,

I don't know how you were able to come by this Benefactor, but I don't want to know either. With this, we'll be able to create the most perfect, prolific fighting force humanity has ever known. We've already identified some special subjects within the EEN to advance humanity. Others on Earth have already been identified and are being monitored for potential candidacy. I'll leave the methods of bringing them in up to you. This truly is a historic day for us as a species.

Farver.

It was only a mere introduction. Flipping through the pages, it was astounding the amount of planning that had already been done. How they would gather subjects, personnel needed to fulfill the project, and the most important one... The location of the Athena sites. More specifically, the system they were to be, or must be located. Lance stuck the file in his ballistic vest. He didn't necessarily want to, but it felt right to take it with him.

Before exiting the office, he looked around the room that was once his creator's. For a split-second, her smiling figure waved to him from the desk chair. A thought occurred to him as he closed the door. It was funny, she was one of the people he most despised, yet Lance wouldn't have gotten here without her. Farver, the man in the suit, the instructors... They deserved to die as much as he did, even if he had a second chance because of them. But more than that, he needed answers. Answers to why he was created. Why he was special. Why him and not someone else. *What do I do with the life you've given me?*

The sound of shuffling brought Lance back out of his thoughts. Peeking around the corner, there were three targets halfway down the hall. Two were foot soldier type. The third in the center had a slightly different appearance. Its movement felt very familiar, like looking at the backs of his squad. The center Vekros stopped and turned around while Lance slid back behind the wall just in the nick of time. The sound of the other two faded down the stairwell. Lance could barely make out the almost inaudible steps of the third. It was hard to tell if it was approaching him or leaving this floor. Eventually, it got quiet with only the sound of a draft somewhere on this floor. Now would probably be the perfect time to get moving again.

Just as Lance turned the corner, his hair stood on end, and he just barely dodged a heavy kick. He was able to slip past and was ready to counterstrike when the Vekros pivoted with a roundhouse kick. Lance jumped back from this attack with an armored boot just passing inches in front of his face. Lance raised the maw to get a shot, but the gun was kicked from his hands. Now he was locked in hand-to-hand combat with whatever Vekros this was. Unsheathing his knife, he lunged for a weak spot in the enemy's armor. The Vekros knocked his arm away right before his knife could impact its underarms. *How can this thing keep up with me? It's like it already knows my movements.*

The Vekros went on the offensive, unleashing a series of kicks and punches. It attacked in a way where Lance couldn't effectively use his knife to get any damage. When he did manage to strike it, the blow would just glance off the armor. It was doing its level best to keep him off-balance, always having to reposition his strikes. Every move the enemy made reminded him so much of others he fought with.

He was getting nowhere by trying to stay out of range of its strikes. Taking a page from the commander's book and doing something unexpected, Lance moved into the attack to get closer to the target. This clearly took the Vekros off guard as the blow of the attack was comparatively weak from the other ones he had dodged. Now he had it right where he wanted it. The Vekros was trying to take a step back as Lance brought the knife around.

Lance stabbed the Vekros up under the ribcage. An audible grunt came from the helmet of the enemy. This time Lance was caught off guard by the Vekros making a sound. It pulled him down with it and the knife slipped out from the wound. Now Lance and the Vekros were locked in a struggle for possession of the knife. The two wrestled on the ground, each with a hand over the handle. The Vekros had the size advantage, and Lance found himself on his back. It managed to get the knife pointed at Lance's head and was steadily pushing down towards him. He searched for anything that could be useful. A shard of glass lay just out of reach, but that would mean letting go of the knife.

Fixing his eyes at the point of the knife, Lance let it go, and his head snapped to the side. The force of the impact centimeters from his ear. He grabbed hold of the glass and jammed it into the side of the Vekros's neck. The thing fell towards the floor, its helmet inches from him, grasping at the shard and the blood started to pour from the wound. Lance didn't let go and started to pull the glass towards him.

"Harro-wer!" The Vekros croaked as Lance cut into the artery. He pushed the armored foe to the side. Then it made sputtering sounds as the life drained out of it. Lance pushed himself into a sitting position and leaned up against a wall exhausted. That was a lot harder than a lot of the fights he had been in. As he sat there going through the fight in his head, the sensation of the hot, sticky blood covering his face. He took his clean hand to wipe it away, looking at his hand, the color of the blood stopped him cold. *Red blood?*

Lance started examining the body a little closer. In terms of size, it was slightly larger than the normal foot soldier with clear musculature, as he already established. The strikes it threw at him were quick and explosive, just like something he learned at Athena. This set off an alarm in his mind and he started searching for clues on the body. He was coming up empty until he flipped over the hand. On top of the armor plate was inscribed... 172.

Those are human numbers. They were written by a human hand. But how? The Vekros don't capture humans. It doesn't make sense.

Then the realization took hold. The fighting style, the reading of his movements, everything that this Vekros did was too human. More than that- It was an operator! It could just be a stretch, and this was all circumstantial at best. Still, everything seemed to fit that it was. Lance began to shake at the thought of killing one of his own. He couldn't catch his ragged breaths as images of other operators flashed in his mind. Each one dead in a more gruesome way than the one before. Lance shut his eyes tightly and slammed a fist into the wall beside him. It was everything he had in him to not scream out.

When Lance thought he was about to lose it, a feminine silhouette outlined by a streetlight edged its way in. He focused on the figure, and the image got clearer. Then he was greeted by that sweet voice and smile. None of the words he could make out, but Lance was sure it was something nice. Some time went by, and Lance was able to calm down and get a clear head. He looked at the body from the corner of his eye, replaying that fight in his mind. Whoever this was, whether they actually were an operator or not, he'll make the whatever Vekros in his path pay for what they did. *What did he call me? Harrower? The Revenant and his Harrowers. Sounds perfect.*

Dusting himself off, Lance picked up the maw and watched over the body once more as if in silent vigil for the fallen warrior, then leaving promptly when he thought he was beginning to waste time. There weren't any enemies immediately in the stairwell, which probably meant the battle upstairs didn't raise any alarms. That fight made him slightly behind schedule. It's about time he got back on track and eliminate whatever the Vekros had in waiting for him.

Lance busted through the door and the two foot-soldiers from before wheeled around at the sudden sound. They were met with one round each into their helmets. Both fell to the floor as he rushed by, their armored bodies clattering over each other. He flew down the next set of stairs and flung open the door to the next floor. There were more enemies here, many backed away in what looked like shock. Lance spent no time dispatching them as well, with a single shot per fighting or retreating Vekros. It made no difference if they were armed or not for they would have done, and did do the same.

The next few floors he cleared in more or less the same manner. The Vekros were ill-prepared for an intruder, more than likely expecting their prized new protector to take care of any that may arise. Well, Lance already put him to rest. No enemy reinforcements came to greet him either. His assault was so sudden and swift that the Vekros couldn't respond before they were nothing but corpses. If he kept up this pace, he would get to the rendezvous well before any of the others could.

Crashing into the server room, it certainly was a target rich environment. Three on the stairs at the far end, seven on a raised area to the right, about the same to the left. This large space had plenty of areas that he wasn't able to see yet, but there could easily be thirty enemies. He noted their delayed response to his presence in part from the many computers running. Lance would have to be careful with his shots. The data was his true target in all of this, Vekros were just his personal objective.

Each of the enemies reached for a sidearm. By the time they had brought them to bear, Lance had already taken down the seven on the right. He decided it was better to stay on the move than wait for them to come to him. It would also make it harder for the Vekros to shoot him. They all stayed roughly in the same positions as he made his way through them, clearing the entirety of the right side of the server room. The Vekros were staying in their assigned areas, making his job a hell of a lot easier. Instead of supporting each other, it seemed their time was better spent protecting a small portion of computers.

Lance went for the central set of computers next. These ones were a little more eager and alert than the last. It didn't matter in the slightest. Lance would go one way and get the drop on one. Another instance he would double back and take out another one from a different direction. It was rinse and repeat. The Vekros were never going to be a match for him, the foot-soldiers were too basic an enemy to be a threat to him. The left and far ends were cleared in a similar manner. All-in-all, it took ten minutes to clear out the entire server room.

Lance listened for the thunderous sound of numerous enemies rushing in from outside, but it was silent. Checking the ammo indicator, it reported that he still had four rounds left in the magazine with one in the chamber, making five. He decided to reload the weapon now and not in the midst of a firefight. Lance found the computer terminal he was looking for shortly after reallocating his ammo. He took out a stick computer and plugged it into the port. The computer responded with a download indicator which quickly left the screen. Then a status bar appeared front and center. This was all the stick's doing, all he had to do was monitor the progress and deliver its contents later.

The bar moved faster than he thought it would considering the amount of data that was stored on these computers. It *was* only picking out predetermined sets of data, likely being locations and strength of the Vekros on this planet and if they were lucky, the surrounding systems as well. It was a waste that was the only thing being retrieved. These servers contained both old EEN files as well as the ones the Vekros had uploaded onto the system once they secured it. With nothing better to do, Lance let his mind wander about the current operation, specifically, the city he was in now and all the towns he would have to pass up.

If the EEN had to come in and eventually liberate these areas, then why wasn't he tasked with sabotage at the very least? It made a lot more sense in the wrong run. In the plans that he saw, this city was on the list to be retaken. Maybe it would benefit the commander and the rest of his team if they had readily available reinforcements instead of having them tied to an area he was totally capable of taking himself. Not to mention that the EEN could recover all this data they were missing, it would be a lie to say he wasn't interested in what he could find out more about Athena.

The computer beeped when the download was finished, and the stick computer clicked out of the port. Lance secured the stick computer and made one final check on his supplies. It wasn't a part of his assigned mission, but he decided he wanted to take out the rest of the Vekros himself. Not just the ones here in Raveset, but in the entire city and in the towns that lay in his path. It was the only consolation he could give for that unknown operator, 172. Lance was going to litter the streets with their corpses.

It was hard to stay in cover when everything was burning. Edward had to admit to himself that it was rather dumb to engage the Vekros in a firefight while still inside a burning hanger. Fio and Olivier were taking turns firing out from under a wrecked Vekros fighter. He was trying to direct their fire visually, not that the bright flames and smoke made things any better. His eyes teared up from straining and smoke irritation. They were still able to take down enemies left and right. He just wanted out of here already!

"Three more coming from the right side of the entrance!" Edward shouted as he rubbed his eyes.

"I'll handle them!" Fio responded with exhaustion.

"I need another mag if you have one!" Olivier requested and Edward, very carefully, tossed one down to him. "Thanks!"

Edward knew that this was a military complex and that it housed hundreds of Vekros, what he didn't know was that they all would come here! He thought blowing something up would be fun, not taking on the brunt of the enemy defense force. It was hard to hear over the roar of the flames, but there was a low grumble that sounded like it was getting louder. Then he saw it. It glinted from the illumination provided by the flames; a Valence was quickly heading towards them.

"Guys, armor inbound! It's gonna get real interestin'!"

The Valence shifted into another gear. Ryder couldn't hear the firefight around the hanger, but he could see shadows moving around the flames. It was still hard to make out which side was friendly, and which wasn't even with the panoramic view. That was the interesting thing about this tank. The EEN tanks had a single computer screen that was connected to a camera that faced one direction with the commander providing the rest of the vision for the driver. The Valence "vision" moved whenever Ryder moved his head. That caught him off guard and took some getting used to.

The figures on the outside were shooting just in front of an open hanger. Those figures were just about on top of another group. Ryder was really hoping that group was his because he was either going to do something really smart or really stupid. He grabbed a plastic charge, reaching back and sticking it to one of the ammo stowage locations behind the driver. Ryder broke off the accelerator and the tank continued to rumble forward. He popped open the driver's hatch and pulled himself out. The outside air, even with a fiery blaze, was much cooler than it was inside the tank. Ryder barreled off the side and sent out a warning.

"Anyone by the hanger, take cover now!" Only a few seconds went by after the warning before the tank blew. The turret tossed into the air and landed several yards away. It took out many of the shadows in that area, and the others were dispatched quickly by small arms from the hanger. Three other shadows came rushing out from the burning hanger.

"Got the message. So glad you can join our little foray." Edward joked though the relief in his voice was evident. Ryder stretched out on the ground.

"I'm glad I hit the right spot. I'm not Lance, so it was a total guess as to where you guys were." Ryder knew it was no time to laze around, but his energy felt drained. **"Rene? Chika? Progress report."**

"We got things handled here." Rene answered.

"What took you so long?" Chika giggled.

"What? How'd you take the control tower already?" Ryder sat up straight looking back at where he left Chika.

"I just did what the commander would do. Play it smart and do something unexpected. In reality, it was a lot simpler

than that." She replied nonchalantly while giving the commander praise.

"Say, you did the same thing too, Ryder. By blowing up a tank in that manner, which wasn't exactly smart, but we'll go with it." Fiorenza pointed out.

"Fair point. I still want to hear exactly how you did it Chika." Explosions could be heard in the not too far distance. One by one, lights went up into the sky. So much for Heike and Misha taking the guns out quietly. To be fair, it wasn't like they were being very subtle over here either. What should have made him mad actually made him smile. Ryder didn't know how it happened, but somehow, they all felt closer and put up with each other's quirks. It was completely different than it was nearly a year ago.

It took some time for everyone to regroup at the control tower. The first rays of light were starting to streak across the sky. Ryder decided the squads would recuperate for a little while, which was also approved by the three captains of said squads. In the meantime, Olivier was tinkering with a transponder that would send out the all-clear and get them resupplied. One thing was clear as everyone went about doing their own thing. It wasn't the same, not having Lance and the commander around. Those two were the glue that held the three squads together. All seemed to revolve around them. If he was honest with himself, Ryder rather preferred Lance so he could get some shots in, but that would have to wait a little longer.

"Got it, the transponder is broadcasting." Olivier fashioned the device to one of the antennae. "We should be expecting a resupply drop in the next hour."

"Good work. All of you did a fine job out there today." Ryder complimented. "Now we just have to get to the rendezvous before our superiors do."

"Hey, not to rain on the wonderful compliment, but you looked so out of character. Like a sentimental old man!" Heike laughed. A'Darrion was trying to hold in his own, but quickly burst into laughter with the captain. Ryder, at a loss for words, just started mumbling incoherently. So much for trying to act as the vice-captain. He was certainly going to make them pay over the next few days.

Intermission III

At Odds

The fan was the perfect white noise for Marilyn to think. She squeezed the area around her temples in an attempt to relieve an excruciating migraine. This wasn't usual for her, rather, it was an abnormality brought on by the high workload of late. To top it off, Marilyn, as director of the Athena Project, had to make a decision on where to funnel resources. This should have been done weeks ago when it was first brought to her attention. Marilyn had just gotten so caught up in her work that it must have slipped her mind despite the constant reminders. Another abnormality.

Funneling resources was the wrong way of putting it. It was more like a decision that would dictate how the EEN would utilize the operators. Marilyn held both profiles in her hand. There were two outstanding subjects even before the procedures. Now both made impressive gains that put all the other operators to shame, well outside her outlooks she made for each one.

The female subject, number two-three-two-one Kirkegaard, was made for this project. Marilyn's agent had picked her up outside the Ribe Cathedral. For a girl her age, she was cunning and avoided the agent for some time. In the end, the promise of food and a safe place to sleep won the girl over. Someone had to be a true monster to lie to a little kid like that. Some things had to be done that way in order to make progress.

Once Kirkegaard was brought in, she had the procedure done immediately. It was a huge gamble not easing the fragile body into a symbiotic state with the catalyst, death was certainly on the table, but the subject survived. The higher ups were especially enamored with this subject, and who wouldn't be, the name practically is the project. The talent was there, the test scores were in the top one percent, field tests showed the subject's durability and intelligence. This one could only be described as a home run.

Marilyn, on the other hand, preferred subject one-nine-four-five Field. In terms of potential, this one had a low floor but high ceiling in sports terms. The things subject one-nine-four-five would be able to accomplish would far outweigh subject two-three-two-one could ever hope to achieve. While it was true that the former subject has tremendous upside, but the latter subject was already on a growth path that would surpass hers. It would take time, much time; Marilyn thought that he would still be the correct choice.

The shrill sound of the phone scared her out of her thoughts. Marilyn thought of just ignoring the call, but if it was the Chief then she would get some "nice" words later. She tossed the papers aside and begrudgingly picked up the phone.

"This is Farver." She yawned.

"Sounds like you've had better days." The voice stifled laughter. Marilyn's eyes widened just a little. She wasn't too keen to speak with this man right now despite going way back.

"Adolf von Schultz, have you been doing well? How's the promotion to director of PONI been treating you?" Marilyn asked unenthusiastically, cradling the phone between her ear and shoulder to continue looking at the profiles.

"Both great." Adolf replied with a tone that hinted his surprise, something that was hard to do with him. "How'd you come by that? I don't remember sending any emails informing you of my position."

"I have my sources considering what I'm doing here and the lack of help from you. It's better to have an information network of my own." Farver said flatly while tracing her finger along a line of a page.

"Sounds like to me that you aren't in the mood for a nice chat today." Adolf sighed.

"Correct, and if you don't have anything important to discuss, then we'll talk another time." Marilyn started to take the phone away from her ear.

"So which subject are you going to pick?" The question rang in Farver's ear. She brought the phone back to her, face reddening in anger.

"How the hell do you know that?! I swear Adolf you drive me crazy when you do this!" Marilyn hissed.

"Now, now, Mari, no need to get mad. I have an information network that far exceeds the one you possess. If you want your people to remain safe, listen to what I have to say." The director of PONI said coolly.

"Are you threatening me?!" Marilyn eyed the phone sharply, knowing that her cutting gaze wouldn't reach him.

"Do you really want to risk in finding that out?" Came a much darker, colder tone.

"Spit it out then." Farver eased back on the attitude. The papers crinkled under her fingers as a result.

"Doctor Farver, between the two subjects, two-three-two-one should be the only option. It already has signs of an ability and is far superior to the other weapons that you have produced. That thing learned seven languages in a matter of months, it fires with the precision exceeding the White Death, and the list goes on. Why are you dragging your feet?"

"I'm considering the other operator. That subject has more potential and is worth the investment. I had gone to great lengths to bring him in for a reason." Marilyn replied as she looked at the picture of one-nine-four-five. She could hear the shuffling of papers on the other side of the phone.

"Yes, I know what you did to get a hold of that subject. Getting the moth- "

"Shut up! Right! Now! I've made my choice and it's going to be him." Doctor Farver was ready to end the conversation, but Adolf growled his disappointment.

"Wrong answer. If you don't go with the female subject, I'll have no choice but to release all of this to the public, and you can say sayonara to your agents." Adolf calmly threatened.

"What? You can't! That would do irreparable damage to the public's view of the EEN. And I already agreed to listen to you so why kill my agents after that?" Marilyn tried to hide her distress to no avail.

"I can do it because I simply can. I'd be seen as someone bringing justice to all of those missing children, some murdered at that. You can only cover this up for so long by yourself. You know as well as me that those parents aren't going to stop searching for their missing kids." Marilyn leaned over the desk horrified. Adolf, only after a short while had gathered this much dirt on Athena Corps. It was only a handful of children that were taken from their parents, the rest really were orphans. If he was willing to go this far, he could fabricate that all of the children were kidnapped by Athena, and she would be powerless against it. The perfect blackmail.

"Fuck you, Adolf." Marilyn muttered.

"I. Want. Your. Answer." The PONI director showed no signs of losing his temper with her. Why would he? He had everything the way he wanted. Marilyn could see his sadistic smile. Feel his cold hands wrap around her throat. His soul as black as the dark space itself. All slowly suffocating her as she grasped into the void.

"Subject two-three-two-one will be... humanity's king." Marilyn replied defeated, her head drooped towards her desk.

"A wise decision indeed and an excellent chess reference. Which reminds me that we need to play a game the next time you come back. One more thing, I'll be making all the decisions for your little project from now on." The phone call ended, and Marilyn was left in silence. She screamed violently as she threw the phone at the wall. *Why Amante? Why'd you have to befriend a monster like him?*

Blaming the Chief wouldn't do her any good. It was her fault too. Neither of them noticed Adolf's darker, twisted side. His view of how things were supposed to be was so skewed that black and white didn't even matter. The wolf had finally cornered the lamb and there was nothing that Farver could do to escape his grasp. All that was left to do was submit to his will.

Chapter IV

Teacher and Pupil

Dust whirled around the shuttle as the doors opened. Lera shielded her eyes when stepping off. The climate reports didn't mention this region would be this dry. It took longer than expected to get planet side, all from working with the other captains of the other ships in coordinating a blockade. An insurance policy against the Vekros that might try and break through to reinforce ground positions. Commander Horstmann walked out from behind a group of loitering soldiers to greet her.

"Welcome to Lion One!" Helen shouted over the shuttle's whine as it took off. Lera had to hold on to her cap so it wouldn't blow away. Helen helped by shielding her from most of the wind. Lion One was a lot nicer than what Lera was using on Verdant Prime. Despite its size, it was easily defensible and the perfect location for headquarters. The only problems she had with it was that it wasn't mobile and nowhere near located to the frontlines. She only planned on staying here for a little while since Helen insisted on her being here.

"Your troops created the fabrications rather quickly. I wasn't expecting the buildings to be ready." Lera complimented while getting a better look at the HQ. It was still a few hours off from midday, but everything was already in order for the major offensive ahead.

"This isn't my first rodeo junior." Helen held open the door to the command center.

"J-Junior?" Lera gave the commander an inquisitive expression. Helen tried her best to look serious but the smile she was trying to hide was evident.

"Let me explain things a little, or something of that nature… Just work with me. What if I said that we were going on a full-scale retreat, and you're tasked with defending the pass. What would you do?" Not understanding why she was being asked this, Lera gave it some thought, noting the Captain James did something similar to her before the battle. This was a scenario that had played out thousands of years before and countless times since.

"If I call, Leonidis stalled the Persians at The Battle of Thermopylae. Things are different in obvious respects, but an ambush that separates the Vekros recon from its main army could blind them. Then we would fight a delaying battle down the canyon, leading them into more ambushes before finally luring the weakened main army to the other side where they could be crushed by a well-prepared defense."

"Wonderful! It's certainly something I wouldn't do, but if things played out that way, it would work. You're always thinking offensively when I was being pretty specific on running away and I like that, not many commanders are willing to make risks."

Horstmann had the look of a fan adoring their favorite celebrity. "I want to know, why reference a battle so ancient? There are way better examples that more closely resemble modern battles."

"That's just if everything goes according to plan. As for why I chose that specific battle, it's by far the most impressive. A force of three hundred stopping thousands in their tracks. I'd say the same thing has been happening here for a while." Lera had to take a step away from the commander's attentive gaze. She still wasn't used to people looking up to her like a senior. Especially in the case of Commander Horstmann who's older and has much more battle experience.

"You have a knack for getting things back on track even if they stray from your original idea. So don't sell yourself short." Helen patted Lera on the shoulder.

"Umm, I think you're still giving me too much credit." Lera was starting to get a little embarrassed by all of this praise. She knew better than anyone that she just had beginner's luck, which was weird to apply to a war situation. That was all it was though... luck.

"Do I? Let's find out then." The doorway that they had to duck under to enter led into what was the combat situation room.

It reminded her so much of the bridge of the Moskva. The difference being that this had more people and no automated systems to guide the crew. The people here had a sense of urgency about them unlike the crew of the Moskva. Instead of a blue light of a planet on the table screen, it was a map of the region they would be striking. The Ceratel Valley.

Before she could get a better look at the map, a familiar face came over and handed her a cup of coffee.

"It's not the frontlines but being back here isn't so bad." Udo Rikimaru stated before taking a sip of his own.

"Major! I didn't think I was going to see you here." Lera greeted him happily.

"Originally that was the case. Commander Horstmann was the one who accepted my request to work alongside you." Major Rikimaru replied as he brought her further into the room. "Wherever you go, I'll go too."

"Having you have my back makes me feel at ease here. Thank you, Major." Lera brought the coffee to her lips and drank in the aroma before taking a sip. A tap on her shoulder released her from her little daydream that was starting to form. When she turned to see who it was, she was surprised to see one of the officers around her age squirming about.

"It- It's pleasure to fight alongside you Commander Kurepina, the Santo della Vittoria!" The female officer saluted, but her shouting drew the attention of other officers and soldiers. It was like fans meeting their favorite sports star as they expressed their excitement and admiration. None of the things they were saying made sense to her but all she could do was go along with it. Once the crowd thinned out, Lera went and hid herself behind Commander Horstmann before any more could come out and say more embarrassing things.

"Why are they calling me that? What does it even mean?" Lera whispered to Helen while making sure no one else was going to approach. A giggle came from the Horstmann in response.

"How could they not? You've become really popular within the military and the homefront, you know." Lera eyed Helen unconvinced by that, which she took note of and continued. "You really don't know, huh. Okay, now if we look at every battle that you partook or lead, it resulted in a victory for us. Kurepina, you may not have realized it, but you're bringing back hope to many that humanity can stand up against the Vekros. It's all from your hard work and ability to read the battlefield the way others can't that got you here now. Do you know how sought after you are?"

"Sought after? What do you mean by that?" Lera perked up from trying to hide.

"Every branch of the EEN, even the United States was vying to get you. It was decided somehow that you would serve in a multi-faceted role because of your talents. Do you know what you got on your final simulation test?"

"I never got the chance to. I was assigned to the Moskva the next day." Lera shook her head.

"The average score of that test is a sixty-three and the minimum to pass is a fifty. Kurepina, you scored a ninety-five. The highest that has ever been recorded on that test since its implementation." Helen waited for Lera's reaction, for which she was sorely disappointed.

"I don't understand why that matters. It's just a score from a simulated battle. What should matter is what I do know to end this war." Lera leaned against a desk. She decided to enlist because she wanted to find a way to end the war and all the suffering that it had brought over the past twenty years. Then the operators came along, and she wanted to end it for them. Now she had all of these people looking up to her- grown adults at that!

I thought I would be alright being under the spotlight again. All there was to do was to fight and win, so why? Why do they see me in that way, like I'm some savior? I'm nothing special and I never was. I'm just another soldier. This isn't like being on stage, so I can't just quit, can I?

"Lera, you may not understand it now, but someday you will. It will be a lot of pressure, that much is certain. You have a good head on those slender shoulders and I'm confident you'll be able to handle that. Even if you don't want to see this, it's a part of you know. It's just part of being a leader." Helen clasped both hands around Lera's. Lera looked into the other commander's eyes and saw the understanding in them, relieving her of some of the nervousness that was building. Horstmann gently released her grip and beckoned Lera to follow.

"Come now, we have a battle to win."

Lera followed silently behind Helen as Udo joined them again. She wasn't fond of this weight that was conveniently and precariously placed on her shoulders. A pinch to her hand allowed her to refocus. This wasn't something she should be worrying about right now. There was a battle that needed her attention. *Maybe Lance will listen... or maybe this isn't something I should be bothering him with.*

I wonder how my operators are faring out there...

"Blöder Hund! Why is this stupid mutt with us?" Heike complained as Dog went after some rodent. They had been taking turns watching and leading Dog with no problems. The only one who couldn't ever gain control was Heike. What made it worse was that she only had him not even ten minutes before this result. Rene wanted to say don't yell at it every ten seconds, but he'd thought the learning experience would be better. Heike did need some kind of hint.

"Lance said in the note that he felt better if Dog was with us. That dog is mostly trained, it's your fault that it doesn't listen to you, Heike." As Rene said that; the thought that Lance taught the dog to not listen to Heike was a distinct possibility.

"I'll take him off your hands!" Evie rushed past Heike who was thanking her profusely. "Come her Dog! Let's play!"

"Evie, we're not here to pla- It's no use." Rene gave up trying to keep things orderly, instead just heaving the rifle sling higher onto his shoulder. Chika tapped his arm playfully and he replied with a slight nod. She ran past him to catch up with Evie. Off to his right, Lek, A'Darrion, and Ryder were busy looking over a virtual map as they walked. They've been pretty busy keeping them on track. Only Fenrir squad walked a few steps behind him. He hadn't really got to talk to them much, and the next town was still an hour's walk. How much he would kill to have a vehicle about now.

"Fiorenza? I heard you're a skilled painter and did Lance's mask." Rene awkwardly started the conversation. The three Fenrir members looked at each other. Rene didn't know what they were communicating about with their eyes, it was quite interesting to watch.

"Please, call me Fae or Fio, though most call me Fio. I'm surprised you knew. I thought that was something between him and I." Fiorenza responded.

"Stonewall spoke of how he learned to paint from you. The brushstrokes were identical to the ones on Lance's mask. That's how I pieced the two together." Rene explained simply as the three Fenrir operators walked in stride with him.

"You make it sound so easy, Captain. Was it that obvious?" Fio asked and looked at the ground disheartened.

"No, that's not it. Your ability to paint is phenomenal. I... just tend to observe things a little more closely than most. It's how I figured out that it was your art style or if someone is behaving how they normally would." Rene looked around for a better example. "The grass for example, it is mostly standing still, but every so often it will move. When it moves, it's light enough that we wouldn't notice and strong enough to where the tips will quiver. Which means that wind speed is four miles per hour, out of the southeast at that."

"Wow! He's right!" Olivier showed the other two the watch on his wrist.

"Hey! Teach us how to do that. Heike doesn't teach us anything cool like that." Edward begged. Rene put a hand to the back of his neck.

"Sure thing. Firstly, respect your captain more. Her combat experience is second to that of Lance in this theatre and is invaluable."

"You throw shade at her too." Edward returned.

"That's different! She's like a sister to me. Anyway, do as I say, not as I do." Rene replied. He really did feel like an older brother for everyone all the time. Not that he was trying for that, it all happened naturally.

"Why's the ground over there rise so sharply?" Olivier pointed over to the left. Stopping a second to take a look, seeing that meant they were closing in on the rendezvous.

"That direction is a canyon along with the Ceratel Valley. We've been running alongside it for some time now, at least two towns back." Rene glanced over at the three men and the virtual map. "The next town should only have a few platoons' worth of Vekros."

Over the past two days, the three combined squads had carved a path through the region. They were dropped deep into enemy territory for a reason, and that was to provide a new point of entry. The military base was the first and most challenging of the targets they had cleared. Challenging was a strong word, still, nothing from this operation made them sweat. After getting the first resupply, they branched out to the surrounding towns and reclaimed them. Then resupplying a second time, they set out for the rendezvous, clearing more towns in their path, leaving a relatively clear way for the follow-up EEN ground troops.

There still was some little clean-up for the ground troops, Rene doubted they got every Vekros position. Then with this last town being taken care of, this region of the continent would be entirely under the EEN's control. Similar actions were being taken on other parts of the continent with all forces converging on a center point. Rene wasn't sure where yet, but hearing snippets of conversation indicated that the Vekros were deeply entrenched at that location.

The group was approaching an intersection with a cluster of buildings. Among the buildings, a steeple-like structure protruded from near the center of the buildings. The charred wreck of a tank sat partway off the road ahead. The state of the structures was in complete disrepair. From here Rene could tell that some of the buildings were structurally unsound. A tough battle had been fought here before.

Dog stopped suddenly; his ears perked up. He then turned around and began to bark at Evie and Chika. Rene spread out his arms to block the Fenrir operators from taking another step forward. Ryder and the other two stopped and watched in confusion. Evie and Chika were on both knees trying to coax the dog over to them. Lek jogged to Evie and Chika, where quick words were passed, then he slowly walked towards Dog. Warning bells went off in Rene's head. They were out in the open, the only cover being a ditch on either side of the road. Instinct took over, somehow grabbing a piece of each Fenrir operator, and dragged them into the ditch on the left side as a rifle crack rang out.

"Get down!" Ryder yelled from somewhere ahead. Another rifle crack followed. Rene thought he heard someone say "hit", he couldn't be sure. Dog came barreling down the ditch and made a stop next to him.

"Stay down. Sniper in the steeple." Rene warned. The Fenrir operators nodded with bellies pressed against the dirt, trying to get their weapons ready. Rene crawled on his stomach to Chika and Evie, who were about twenty yards away. They must have backtracked before diving down. When he reached them, Evie had the barrel of her own sniper rifle trained at the steeple.

"Are you okay?" Rene tapped the back of Chika's leg, and she waved him up.

"Yeah, we made it down here just fine. Ryder's group and Heike both managed to get down too." The sniper fired again, and Chika pushed Rene's head nearly into the dirt. Evie returned fire and cursed when she didn't hit anything.

"Where's Lek?" Chika eyes darted at the road then back to him.

"I don't know. He was right behind us, maybe Lek dove to the other side of the road?" Chika suggested.

"Ryder? Please tell me you have eyes on Lek?" Rene pleaded.

"Negative, Cap."

Rene gritted his teeth, knowing what likely happened and hoping it wasn't true. He should have realized a lot sooner that something was wrong. This little unincorporated area wasn't marked on their map. They should have taken a different path, or at least have been a bit more cautious moving in on this place.

"Lek! Where are you?" Rene called out. After a few nerve-raking seconds, a pained groan came from the road. *Damn it!* They weren't in an ideal situation, and if Lek could hold on, they could take out the sniper and get him patched up. "Hang on! We'll get you outta there!"

Rene dared to lift his head to try and see how far Lek was from his side of the road. He ducked when his spider sense went off and a round zipped into the dirt behind him. Chika tensed up beside him when that round had gone by. There wasn't any way that that he was going to bring Lek down here when a sniper and them trained in. The operators were going to have to flush out the sniper or Evie had to pinpoint and kill it.

"Listen up. We have to close in and flush this guy out once Evie locates it and provides us with some cover fire. Ideally, it would be better if she killed it." Rene informed.

"I can try, but this one is really good." Evie replied tensely.

"We'll close in from the right side. The closer we get, the better the shots the sniper has though." Ryder commented.

"Should be fine once we get to the buildings, just be careful and be quick." Rene started to creep forward. **"Guess it will come down to who is faster, that things trigger finger or us."**

"Don't forget about *my* trigger finger." Evie added. Rene would have preferred if Evie took out the sniper before they would have to make a break for the cover of the buildings. The destroyed tank along the main road was going to provide enough cover for him to slip in the village. Then the buildings themselves would allow them to close the distance and make that sniper uncomfortable. Rene and Chika crawled through the ditch; they would be flanking from the north. Meanwhile, Ryder and A'Darrion would approach from the south side. Heike was going to support Evie as a spotter from wherever she was hiding while the three Fenrir operators hung back as support. Once the sniper was taken out, they could provide emergency first aid for Lek.

A couple of rifle shots had stopped them in their tracks a few times. After each series they continued to push forward. They were only near misses so far, uncomfortably close near misses. Then the distinct sound of Evie's rifle would sound in response. Unfortunately, they were misses themselves as no report of a confirmed hit came in. At the rate they were going, it was cutting way too close to help Lek.

There wasn't any more time to lose, Rene had to take this thing out now! As soon as he got up, Rene went into a full sprint. The reports of two rifles firing quickened his pace. He dove under the wreck of the tank and the firing stopped. Checking on the others' progress behind him, it looked like he was the only one to take the opportunity to rush to the buildings. He crawled out from the other side of the charred hull and ducked behind an alleyway. There was a lot of rubble that made him have to watch his footing, slowing him down. The last thing Rene needed was to sprain an ankle or inadvertently cause one of these barely standing buildings to collapse. Not that it was too likely, but he wasn't willing to take that chance.

Rene peeked around a corner of a building. Just as he had planned, he was on the north side of the steeple. It looked like a religious building of some kind, hence why it had that structure. Rene did not see Ryder and A'Darrion where they were supposed to be. He was going to have to go off script and hunt the sniper by himself, or at least till the other two showed up. For a split second, Rene thought he caught sight of the sniper in a blown-out window.

He waited approximately ten seconds to be sure that he wasn't spotted. Rene crossed the open square that was reminiscent of old war photos he had seen. Gently pushing open one of the large, ornate double doors; he cautiously stepped in, noting the inside of this place was as much of a wreck as the surrounding structures. There was a gaping hole in the ceiling, it looked to be done by a lighter artillery round as evidenced by the crater in the center of the space. To the right of the entrance was a knocked down door with a staircase. That's where his little sniper buddy would be.

Rene crept up the creaking wooden stairs. Each tentative step could alert the Vekros of his presence. A rifle crack echoed down the stairwell. That was good for him, as long as it was distracted, he could get to and kill it. He was hoping that no one else would get hit in the meantime. They just needed to hold out a couple minutes at most.

When Rene rounded the corner, there it was. The Vekros sniper. It was coming down the stairs as he was going up. Both opponents stopped, shocked to have come face-to-face with an enemy so soon. The enemy sniper went to raise his rifle at Rene. Rene used a heavy kick that sent the sniper out of a convenient hole in the wall. Not being able to keep his balance, Rene began to fall backwards. He tumbled down two flights of stairs before he was able to catch himself. It was only a short fall, but it still left him battered and bruised. Rene slowly got back on his feet, weapon nowhere in sight. His helmet came off too as he ran his hand through his hair where the helmet should have been. Maybe he should have strapped it on. Rene painfully went back to the hole in the wall and looked down. Lying there was the awkwardly bent body of the Vekros sniper.

"This is Lycoris speaking, sniper has been taken care of." Rene looked out towards the road. That little sprint turned out to be a lot farther than it looked from below. He was luckier that he didn't get shot himself.

"I saw. Applying emergency first aid. Y-You should probably get down here quickly." Heike's downturn tone was like a stab to the gut. Rene wiped sweat with a clenched fist from his forehead, then went back down the way he came. As he walked through the area, the utter lack of bodies or equipment was puzzling. Sure, the battle that was fought here was a very long time ago, but there should be more remnants than just a destroyed tank.

If the Vekros thought near the same as humanity, did they also take whatever was left on the battlefield? Not just to recycle equipment, but to better understand the enemy's capabilities and technologies? It would explain some things to some degree. This line of thinking brought itself even more questions. Why would the Vekros do that only here? On every other planet that Rene had been to, the Vekros couldn't care less what humanity had or did. So, what was on Kanto-IV that had caught their attention? Or what made them change?

Rene could see everyone else sporadically gathered around Lek. Their heads dropped, backs were turned to him besides Heike, whose sleeves were rolled up and hands and forearms covered in blood. She saw him coming over intercepted him halfway with an unexpected hug. Caught off guard, Rene could only slowly wrap his own around her, realizing what this meant. He looked up to the sky for a second before looking back at Heike, her usual confidence shattered.

"I'm sorry Rene, I tried." Heike's voice wavered. It had been a very long time since he saw her like this. He pushed her away lightly , but couldn't quite look her in the eyes.

"You did what you could." Rene put a comforting hand to her head, steeling himself for what was next. He walked over and knelt next to Lek, whose breaths of become ragged. The wound pierced right through his clavicle, in a spot where the vests didn't provide protection. That sniper had excellent aim, paired with whatever ammunition type, did a lot of damage. He felt Chika's hand gently squeeze his shoulder.

"Lek, we got the sniper. We'll take a short break before we move on to the rendezvous point." Rene said quietly. Lek's eyes fluttered open; his hand reached out for Rene's, grasping against the dirt. Rene took it in his as Lek began to speak.

"Is... every... right? Must... help." Lek struggled to say, his grip growing weaker with every strained breath.

"Yeah, they're fine. Don't worry. You took a nasty hit, but you'll pull through. We got it from here." Rene choked up on the last sentence.

"Real...ly?" Lek looked up at the sky relieved. Lek's hand began to slip away, Rene held it tighter to him, his throat tightening.

"Yeah. Just rest up. You can cook up a big meal later. Just rest now. You did well. I'm proud of you, Lek." A small, meek smile formed on the man's lips, but the Lek didn't return it. His lifeless eyes left looking to the sky. Lek's cold, bloodied hand slipped away from Rene's now coated in scarlet. The man that lay before him didn't look like Lek anymore, that admiring gaze was gone. Rene bowed his head, tears streaming down his face. Even after doing this time and time again, it still hurt just as bad. Chika's hand brushed away the tears on his blind side and she wrapped her arms around him. He appreciated her effort, but he was lost in his own thoughts, wondering what he could have done differently. There was something that was till in Lek's hand. Reaching out, Rene took the item from him. Rene opened up his own hand, the polished steel gleamed with blood. He could barely read the inscription.

Lek Diskul

#495

Shockwave

Rene tightened his grip on the chain of the dog tag. His first subordinate, student, would never be forgotten.

"Hot" Lera squeaked, shooting a hand up to cover her mouth.

"Everything alright?" Helen asked.

"Yeah, I just burnt my tongue. I guess I didn't let it cool long enough." Lera set the cup down missing her iced coffee. Though something did feel off when it happened.

Lera kept her attention fixed on the big screen, taking glances at the six smaller ones every once in a while. The smaller ones contained the data on the units that were heading into battle. The big screen was the live feed coming in from a drone. What she was seeing was the ninety-seventh armored division rolling along. Helen said she couldn't be in the frontlines for this one. She wanted Lera to gain some experiences in the rear in the heart of the information suite. It was nicer to have eyes all over the place. There was so much to see, rather, a different perspective that showed the bigger picture of the battlefield.

"Good luck, Commander Kurepina." Helen told her with a wink. She would command the rest of the forces while Lera focused on the tougher enemy.

"Thanks. You too Commander Horstmann." Lera returned the energy. She brought her attention back to the main screen. The ninety-seventh just entered the Ceratel Valley. It was only the recon elements. The armored cars moved down the single road. Behind them would be one-hundred and sixty tanks that would clash with the Vekros tanks that were in this region. Wherever those were hiding.

The ninety-seventh was just like any other standard armored division. It was equipped with four different tanks. The first was the heavy tank, the H1 Erdenbrecher. The medium tank was the M13 Carcajou. Then there was the tank destroyer, the T7 Frelon. Finally, the main battle tanks, which was the staple of the EEN, the MBT-9 Girard. The MBTs stayed at the top of the rise, using their excellent gun depression to watch the valley below. Lera gave them a strict order not to charge until the Vekros closed within the bottom of the hill and there was hardly a present threat. Except, there were no enemy tanks in sight. For all she knew, they could be driving straight into a trap.

"Send drone three over those trees." The visual feed began to move in that direction. Nothing seemed out of place. At least it was meant to look like that. "Lower altitude, get right on those treetops."

The trees grew larger and larger until the sky was no longer in frame. The drone moved along the leading edge of the trees with nothing. There! The large silhouette of a tank. It was unmistakable. The Vekros were going to ambush them. A rocket appeared on screen with a simultaneous "signal lost".

"Squad One! Advance towards Delta Twelve. Recon, pull back. Spread out and keep an eye on the tree line!" The MBTs crested over the rise and drove down the open ground of the valley. Emerging from the tree line were twenty-four Valence medium tanks. The MBTs were more than capable of handling medium tanks. There still were three times the amount of Squad One.

It was hard to make out, but there definitely were anti-tank guns lying in wait behind those mediums. As long as the MBTs didn't show their sides and rear, those guns shouldn't pose much of a problem. It's not like she didn't have the same idea with tanks waiting to rain fire from above. The EEN and Vekros tanks engaged each other in the open. Not only that, the Vekros AT guns also opened up. Lera wanted so badly to micromanage each individual unit's movement. This required her to put her trust in the officers of each unit to coordinate their troops. She just had to keep the flow of the battle going at the pace she wanted. Things would be so much simpler if she was up there with those tanks.

The Vekros were hemorrhaging their armor. Another six Valence tanks had been taken out. Things were going easy. Squad one had taken no casualties and only some light damage. The skirmish here will be over soon.

"Commander. Vekros armor approaching from the south. Fifty units identified." An officer informed.

"Squads Two and Three, head to Echo Four. Use those hills to your advantage." The screen switched to a view of those two squads. Echo Four was a perfect position. The gun depression allowed the MBTs to fire almost with impunity. If the Vekros were to land a shot, it more than likely would bounce due to the extreme angle of the armor.

"Squad One is getting hit with rockets."

"Send in infantry support. Keep the advance moving." Squad Two and Three began firing down on the enemy tanks. They staggered their fire so at least two tanks were always firing. The closest targets were prioritized so they could maintain the high ground.

One of the tanks went too far forward, resulting in a track getting blown off. Lera watched in agony as two of the crew jumped out and got to work repairing the track. That tank was being focused fired by what little tanks were left to oppose the two squads. After what felt like years, the track was repaired, and the tank backed away. Lera's foot had played a steady beat throughout the entirety of that skirmish. So far, they have found eighty enemy tanks, most now burning wrecks. Half the enemy force was out there still. The advance had them almost through the Ceratel Valley. Surely the Vekros didn't use half their forces as a sacrifice to retreat. That line of thinking wouldn't lead anywhere. The Vekros never retreated, but they also weren't tacticians by any stretch. Still, where could they have gone?

"Casualties reported. Enemy tanks are at our rear!"

"Get Squad Four and Five back there!" Lera ordered.

"They won't make it in time." Lera looked at their ETA. As fast as the MBTs could travel, it would take them twenty minutes to support the defense. The area would be overrun by then.

"Have Hunter One through Three intercept. Have them hold those tanks back until support arrives." They didn't have a drone in that area, so Lera had to settle for dots on a map. Too bad she couldn't scramble any air support either, those resources were tied up at different fronts.

The T7 Frelon was a very light and nimble machine, albeit it had very little in the way of armor. It drew inspiration from French designs where the amount of armor mattered not in modern warfare, as any round would still be able to penetrate. With that little armor, it was able to fire and relocate rather quickly for a machine of its size. Even though the tank destroyer had little protection, it did have teeth. The 120mm gun is no longer the top gun it used to be, yet it was still capable of piercing the front of the Valence armor. The problem here was that it was three against possibly eighty.

If she felt nervous just watching Squad Two and Three, Lera waited with bated breath with these three singular tanks. The only help that Hunters One, Two, and Three had was whatever the support units stationed there could provide. It would only amount to AT rockets, but those were better than nothing at this point. The three hunters split off in three different directions. This area had a lot of rocky spots for them to hide. Tactically, the hunters had the advantage in this terrain. The Frelons began their hunting. They targeted tanks that stalled behind their groups. This was going to be too much still.

"Do we have any available squadrons to provide air support?" Lera asked aloud.

"Yes, but they're returning from a mission the- "

"Scramble them back into the air, ASAP." Lera interrupted.

"Yes Commander."

It was a stroke of luck that there was any available squadron. The ninety-seventh just had to hold out for ten minutes. The hunters were tearing up the battlefield. The hit and run tactic they were using was proving to be effective. When the Vekros tried to regroup, those three tank destroyers would come at them from an unexpected direction and disrupt their coordination. One of looked like it was traversing and jagged rocks! What those three were doing right now was exactly what she would be doing if she was in their position.

"Friendly aircraft have entered the detection zone. Thirty seconds until fire mission." A female officer looked up from her screen.

The central screen panned to the largest group of Valence tanks were located. Explosions ripped through the formation one after the other. The squadron of S-2 Swordfish had dropped five-hundred-pound bombs right on top of those tanks with expert precision. Lera had no idea if they were guided or unguided, just glad they turned up when they did and were great hits otherwise. The squadron turned around for another pass and opened up with their revolving cannons. The rounds pierced right through the top of the tanks like butter. Right on cue, Squad Four and Five arrived on the scene to help the three hunters mop up the stragglers. A quick look at the other parts of the Ceratel Valley showed much of the same. The battle was coming to a close.

"What are our casualties?" Lera inquired.

"Figures are showing more than five-hundred and forty, with twice the number of wounded so far. Official numbers will be posted later."

Lera balled up her fist. Even after a battle where they had the advantage, it cost them this much. It was way more than Lera had planned on losing. If she was out there with them, then there wouldn't have been any losses. On top of that, she was expected to win. Of course, she was going to; but at what cost in the end?

"You did well, Commander. Be proud of your victory." Commander Horstmann came over and lightly elbowed Lera's arm.

"How can I when I lost so many?" Lera mumbled so only Helen could hear her. She gave Lera a look that was sympathetic.

"That was one comment that was a negative on your simulations. You try too hard to limit casualties. Now that's all fine a goal to have, but you can't expect that from yourself. You'll end up running yourself ragged. Trust me, it's terrible to lose your soldiers, I know this all too well. But as a leader, you have to make those tough calls. War doesn't play fair; it only takes what it can get its hands on."

Lera didn't like any of those words. They actually made her sick to hear. To her, that was the same as giving up. That it was okay to want to lose those soldiers. She wasn't going to do that with her operators, so she wasn't going to do the same with anyone else. Lera was part of this war too, and she'd be the outlier that didn't play by War's rules.

"Keep your head up, don't let your troops see you down. Ever." Helen lifted Lera's chin and patted her on the back before walking back to her post.

After eleven hours of fighting in and around the Ceratel Valley vicinity, the troops under Horstmann's command were now on the move with a victory under their belt. Lera was riding in her command car, mulling over those words the Horstmann spoke. They toiled in her mind like a lion in a cage. The entire day had worn her out. Not even a coffee could provide her enough energy anymore. Right now, she was headed for the rendezvous she gave the operators. Lera brought along a small convoy, a few trucks and armored personnel carriers. It was enough to resupply and transport them to their next objective. This time though, they'll all be in this fight together. She felt the vehicle decelerate.

"Huh? Major? Are we already here?" Lera asked groggily, stretching her arms over her head.

"Yeah, but we aren't the first ones." Rikimaru laughed a little. Confused by his meaning, she stepped out of the vehicle. Lying atop the roof of a house, book in hand, was Lance.

It took a few minutes for her to get to the house. There was a ladder set up against the house. Lera climbed up the ladder onto the roof. Lance didn't take his eyes off the book and continued to read when she sat next to him. She just watched the sunset that was on full display. Purples and pinks mixed in with fading orange. It was like this for a few minutes before the thump of a book closing stopped her daydream.

"How was it?" Lera asked. Lance closed his eyes and sat the book down next to him.

"Hmm. The plot was very engaging. The characters were pretty developed too. I still ended up predicting the ending, but I did enjoy the story." He patted the book.

"That's not what I meant?" Lera rolled her eyes. Lance sat up and looked at the sunset.

"It went fine, Commander. There's no reason to worry about my end." Lance replied confidently.

"It's my job to worry. I wouldn't know how to keep the others getting along otherwise. Anyway, you were supposed to be the last one here." She cocked her head just a little to watch him, but she was met with him watching her instead.

"Uh! Hey, what's that look for?" Lera looked back at the horizon.

"You look a little tired Commander. Something's on your mind." Lance read her so easily.

"Is it that obvious?" Lera pouted.

"No, you are good at hiding things. It's just a skill I learned from Rene." Lance scooted over slightly. "Better just say it, Commander. I can't have you getting distracted when we need you the most."

"Is it wrong that I want to save everyone? Trying to prevent soldiers from dying?" Lera questioned, still looking off in the distance. Lance remained silent, making Lera think he might disagree too.

"It's not wrong to try and do that. I've done the same in the past. Just don't let the hard battles get to you." Lance expressed after a while.

"That last part doesn't make any sense." Lera yawned. She felt her cap lift from her head, with Lance firmly setting it on his. "I didn't say you could take that."

"True. You wouldn't be able to do this." Lera felt her head rest against something firm.

"I don't know what you're talking about." She yawned again. Lera found it hard to keep her eyes open anymore. Maybe it would be fine to rest her eyes. She'll have to scold Lance later...for...

There was hardly any light left in the sky. Lance's eyes were focused on the girl peacefully sleeping on his shoulder. Her soft breathing was a sweet lullaby that was making him tired as well. Even with the low light, her amber hair seemed to shine still. It did surprise him that she didn't put up more of a fight. He was relieved that it turned out this way. Knowing the commander, she hadn't rested once since the start of this operation. If it was her job to worry about him and the operators, then it was his job that she took better care of herself.

Eventually she woke up after a little rest unsure of why she was leaning against him. They left the roof and Lera excused herself for the rest of the night. As that was happening, Lance picked up on the operators' presence as they followed along the road Lera had come in on earlier. They weren't in their typical formation and were dragging a cart behind them. He watched them go to the medical tent, and Ryder was pointed to Lance. He reached Lance at plopped down to Lance's right. Lance glanced down at his vice-captain.

"I heard from the Major that some towns and a city was completely cleared of hostiles. Wonder who did that." Ryder took a drink from his canteen of water. "Nice hat by the way."

"I got tired of looking at them, so I got rid of them." Lance took off the Commander's hat so he could return it after this conversation. "How'd it turn out for you?"

Ryder emptied the canteen. Then he sat there in silence for a long time. Lance waited patiently since he had something else to occupy his mind. The man next to him sighed.

"The commander looks like she's doing fine." Ryder tried to distract.

"Don't change the subject. What happened? Lance persisted.

"Lek is gone." Ryder said softly. Something caught in Lance's throat. That wasn't something he was expecting to hear. He knew splitting up from the others was a bad idea, but he was sure that they had everything under control. Lance would let it be for now.

"It hit us all hard. Rene especially had been hit hard by this." Ryder continued as he dragged his canteen across the ground. "It was our negligence that caused this. We should have suspected a sniper, but- "

"Get some rest, Ryder. I'm sure you guys did your best with what information you were given." Lance replied after Ryder had stopped talking. Ryder got up and threw his canteen against a building, hands rubbing the back of his head. It didn't look like Ryder was fairing much better the Rene.

Lance stayed and was thinking of all that needed to be done now. He was still surprised to hear this. Lek was by far the most improved of the non-captains. Lek was on track to become one himself, he just had the knack for it and was eager to learn. Now Lance had to adjust squad formations, supply numbers, and other nonsense. That was something for a different day. Right now, he just wanted to get ready for tomorrow's battle. Those Vekros are going to pay.

Chapter 5

Bloody Potzlan

Order 3407

By the will of the Emperor, all forces stationed at Planet 1207-B are not to give any ground to the enemy.

The enemy shall not interfere with The Project.

Rejoice, that the Emperor believes in your prowess and drive back the harrowers from the planet.

The Emperor's master plan is underway. Prove your usefulness and you shall be rewarded.

"Mason! Get a move on! Take point!" With all the shooting and explosions going on around him, it was hard to focus and pick out the sarge's words. Mason was still feeling rattled after watching Perry get shredded before ever going through the door of the last building. Was he next?

"Yes, sarge!" Pvt. Mason took over Perry's position. The sarge and the rest of the squad lined up behind Mason. Hugging the wall of the building, Mason guided the squad around the corner of the street towards the doorway of the next building. They had to jump over a few craters on their way; Mason couldn't believe how war-torn this city had gotten over a few days. Mason got himself set while the rest of the squad took cover along the walls on either side. A tap on his shoulder was the signal to breach.

Stepping up to that doorway was like stepping up to the plate in baseball. Only that being here was much more terrifying. Mason's legs felt like jelly. The acrid smell of smoke and far worse filled his lungs. Something lodged in his throat and the urge to cough was staved off by the threat of the Veks. He took a few deep breaths, raised his leg and kicked in the door in one hit.

Not even three steps in upon entry, pain ripped through Mason's abdomen. His buddies were stopped at the door as SMG fire prevented them from entering. Mason collapsed in the corner of the room a few feet from the door. He tried to set himself up to defend himself and wait for help, but each movement brought only pained grunts and no progress. Since he couldn't get up, he felt around where the pain was most intense. There felt like three entry wounds, the bottom of his vest was shredded not being able to protect him from such close-range fire. Mason didn't think it was going to end like this as he bled out in the corner. As he was resigning himself to his fate, the window beside him burst into shards. A masked man barrel rolled and emptied a clip into the room ahead of him. The masked man came around and grabbed the collar of Mason's vest.

"Hold on, I'm getting you out." The masked man huffed. The sunlight hit his eyes with a bunch of hands grabbing at him, carrying him away from the fighting. Mason looked back, the masked man was walking away, looked back for a second, the disappeared into the darkness of the building.

Running over rubble was always such a familiar feeling. Bullets flew in from many directions as they dodged from cover to cover. It wasn't like there wasn't ample cover since Rene was in a partially collapsed theater. A'Darrion hung back doing his level best to use suppressive fire. Olivier was steps behind Rene as they sprinted along. The two stories above had Vekros spread out on them. Rene managed to slip onto the stairs to get to the second floor. Unfortunately, the inside wall was blown out, so he wasn't safe from enemy fire. Olivier slid right into Rene, and he pushed the newcomer's head down as holes lined the spot that he would have been at.

They waited for a lull in the incoming fire before moving up the stairs. The progress was gradual in no part from the shear amount of fire they were receiving. Rene leaned out and quickly aimed his assault rifle, firing down the balcony. When he needed to reload, Olivier took over. After the second floor was clear, it was on to the third. Rene passed by the doorway for the second floor to continue up the stairs followed by Olivier. The wall here was reasonably intact besides a few bullet holes and chips. They repeated what they did for the second floor for the third. At the end of that, Rene and the other two had been here for almost an hour clearing this theater.

"Blitz Nine, we are clear. I repeat. We are clear." Rene spoke into the air with his finger at his ear for the comms.

"Good work. We're moving up to the next block." Rene rubbed the back of his neck in an attempt to get a knot out. A'Darrion had his light machine gun partially taken apart.

"What happened there?" Olivier asked from behind Rene. A'Darrion glanced up from his work for half a second.

"Too much dust getting kicked up. It was only a matter of time before it jammed." A'Darrion wiped down the different parts.

"We'll take a short break before going to the next block." Rene plopped down next to a pillar, taking out a dehydrated rations bar. It wasn't the greatest thing ever, its only job being to provide energy and nutrients. They usually had something the Lek had made ready. That was a change Rene was going to struggle to get used to, not having him around.

"I don't know if you guys saw this or not, anyway, this city looks a lot different from when we started our attack." Olivier stated while tearing off the wrapper of his rations.

"I'm not used to this environment. Same with Ryder. We weren't made to travel with armies. We were made to go into enemy held territory and destroy them inside-out." A'Darrion answered while putting his gun back together.

"Eh? Okay... I guess that counts." Olivier looked at Rene for his comment.

"The Vekros dug themselves in like moles. That is already strange by itself, which is why we took such drastic measures as bombing this place and fighting on every block. To piggy-back of A, he's only describing the ever-changing role of the operator." A'Darrion made a disapproving sound at Rene's last statement. He couldn't entirely blame the guy either. It was drilled into them that they were to fight with no support, and they were the key to victory. It can cause some to have an identity crisis when they were told one thing but are doing another.

Olivier got up and walked over to one of the many blown out windows in what used to be a lobby. That was easily the longest conversation that any of them have had since Lek passed. Olivier was the type to try and lighten the mood and he'd been doing that since he was put with A'Darrion and Rene. His problems were A'Darrion was not a conversationalist and Rene didn't feel like he processed it all yet. He appreciated the effort, to say the least, he just needed a little more time was all. A'Darrion put the last piece of his gun on.

"Let's hop to it boys. We got another block to hit." Rene projected. Rene picked up his rifle and waited for the other two at the front entrance. They would have to skirt around this backside if this theater, not knowing if the buildings on the other side had enemies in them yet. The Vekros had a tendency to reoccupy places if they were left untouched after a while. It was a constant press forward scenario because if the EEN didn't, they'd find cleared out areas no longer clear.

"I got point." A'Darrion stepped out, LMG at the ready. Rene followed him out with Olivier five steps behind. The three operators rounded the theater and made it to the target block without incident. Going through proper operating procedure, A'Darrion would bust the door down, Rene went in first followed by Olivier and swept the structure. Each consecutive building the searched without encountering anything didn't sit right with Rene.

Before he knew it, they had gone up and down the block without finding a single Vekros. Besides being bombed out, there were no signs of a fight in this area. Blitz Nine certainly didn't let them know that this area was fine. How far ahead did Blitz get? He was supposed to be working in conjunction with Rene's team. Rene switched his earpiece to the EEN's open channel.

"We are requesting assistance! Unknown enemy unit- We need assistance at Forty-eighth and Uver streets!" Blitz's voice almost blew Rene's eardrum, he was screaming so loud.

"Lycoris here. Hang tight for a couple minutes." Rene replied. He took over the lead, listening for the closest source of gunfire. It was hard to tell with all the other firefights going on, Rene could just tell where to go after hearing an explosion to his front left somewhere ahead. Rene spread out his arms and pointed twice to let Olivier and A'Darrion know to spread far apart. He didn't have the time to stick with general signals. The closer they got, the louder the sound of gunfire, crumbling, and thrashing about. An armored car came rolling down the street, Rene attempted to stop them by waving his hands. The vehicle sped right by without acknowledging the operator's presence. All he could do was follow its path and hope it wasn't dire up there. Rene had tried to stop that armored car not because he wanted to hitch a ride, but the hairs on his arms stood on end. He picked up the pace, it may not be the smartest thing having no idea what they were running in to. Blitz would want him there sooner rather than later and Rene was of the same mind.

The clamor of metal-on-metal wrenching sound went in a crescendo. Rene turned the corner- *Shit!* He fell hard on his back to avoid the flying armored car from before. It rolled unevenly right over him and slammed into the buildings that lined forty-eighth before exploding. Rene didn't need to look back to see if the other two were fine as they pulled him back to his feet. In front of them, was a monstrosity Rene really didn't want to engage with. A quadruped armored figure took two steps towards them, stopped, and steam blew out from the rear legs. The body was a metallic blue oval-shaped pod, unlike other Vekros they've fought. This thing didn't have any protrusion that resembled a head, instead having three glowing blue lights in the front that blinked on and off like an eye would blink.

"Spread out!" Rene yelled as an autocannon raised from the top of the quadruped. Each man dove in a different direction as the ground they were just standing in was marred by cannon fire. Rene pulled the pin on a grenade and threw it over his head. A distinct pop from the grenade allowed him to peek his head out from cover. The smoke was able to blind the sensors of the quadruped. He had limited time before the quadruped started moving towards them.

"Focus on its joints! Take out the legs!" Rene barely finished before the quadruped emerged from the smoke and peppered his position. A'Darrion and Olivier returned fire, the sound of rounds pinging off the metal. The whine of the autocannon rotating let Rene know it was his turn to fire. It was going to take more than that. Rene jumped up and sprinted toward the quadruped. Running at this speed made his shots go wide.

The quadruped continued to fire at someone else, raising its leg to attack Rene. He hopped to the side, losing his aim. The heavy thud of the leg hitting the ground vibrated the spot with enough force that Rene nearly lost his balance. More rifle fire from the windows to his right let him know that Blitz was still there somewhere. Rene pulled the pin on another grenade and found the air intake. He jumped up and held to the belly of the pod with one hand while stuffing the grenade with the other. Once he felt it was secure, Rene let go and sprinted to cover. The bottom of the quadruped blew out, the machine wobbled back and forth, eventually buckling towards the ground.

"Stay down! It's not done!" Rene shouted before anyone could get over to it. Ten seconds later, the quadruped exploded with a concussive blast. Rene felt the shockwave go right over him along with the heat. He took some time to catch his breath, it wasn't every day that he did something stupid like that. Lance's fighting ability must have rubbed off on him some, or lack of judgement.

"Are you alright Lycoris?" A wounded soldier stepped into Rene's vision. The soldier walked with a limp, his right sleeve was torn and bleeding as well as another wound that bled down his face. Rene quickly got up and started to check where he put his emergency bandages.

"I could ask you the same thing, Blitz." Rene found the bandages and wipes, tearing off what was left of the other man's sleeve to clean the wound and apply bandages. He would do the same for Blitz head of course.

"I've been worse. This is nothing compared to what happened to me on Ois." Blitz gritted his teeth as Rene roughly cleaned the wounds.

"That makes you- "

"Yeah! Pretty old compared to you gazelles!" Blitz interrupted. Blitz then used his free arm and pointed over at the twenty-foot-wide crater, where his squad and Blitz gathered around. "Anyways, how'd you know about that thing?"

"The Quadsteer? I've fought plenty of them before on other missions. This is the fastest time of killed one of them. The self-destruct happens whether the pilot wants it to or not, so we have no idea what it's like on the inside." Rene moved on to Blitz head wound.

"Quadsteer?" Blitz voice mocked.

"Hey now, I didn't name it. Some other operator named it because it has four legs and likes to charge as the armored car crew found out, unfortunately. Blitz, your special forces, right? How does a Ranger squad get beat up this badly?"

"Tch! Fine, I'll say it. It was wrong of me to go on ahead without you guys." Blitz placed his helmet back on when Rene was finished. Blitz Nine could be stubborn but that didn't mean he wouldn't admit when he was wrong. He was one of the few regs that Rene had hit it off with once the commander integrated them into the regs environment. The mission for them was halted until they could get Blitz and his men back to safety. Rene wondered how the others were fairing out there.

Evie lay prone on the roof of the four-story brick building. She had been here for so long that the butt of her sniper felt like it had left an imprint and her shoulders ached. She had been in this position for almost two hours providing overwatch for the regs below. The first half of that had plenty of action, this last half on the other hand was very quiet for her. The Vekros must have wised up and stayed hiding in their holes. These were the only missions Evie had been assigned to for the duration of her time in this hellhole of a city. There was so much death and fatal wounds she saw that would last her a lifetime.

She wasn't alone on top of this roof getting baked alive. Ryder was somewhere off to her right side. While they were here, the others were all split off in different areas of the city. Lance was where the heaviest of the fighting was, at his own insistence and reluctance of Kurepina. A'Darrion, Olivier, and Rene were also in the vicinity to Lance. Evie had no way of knowing the status of them or the others, but she was sure they were fine.

"Evie. I have some water here." Ryder said with the sound of a canteen being placed next to her.

"Naw, I don't want it yet." Evie kept her eyes fixed through the scope. Some regs came out of a building unscathed; their faces looked calm, relaxed, but their body language displayed fear. That ticked her off a little. Didn't they know they were in good hands with her watching over them?

"Drink something will ya. You haven't had anything since last night." Ryder insisted with his patience wanning.

"I hear you, but I don't want to take my eyes off spot." Evie fought back.

"Fine! Have this and drink something already." Evie felt a metal straw placed at her slightly parted lips. Now she finally drank something. "Ya know you piss me off sometimes."

"You make it so easy to." Evie laughed. All she got was a snort in response. It was his fault, if Ryder didn't want her to mess with him then he should keep volunteering to be her spotter. It wouldn't be too long before she would have to relocate. The regs had almost cleared this street. Compared to other squads she covered; they had few casualties. All in part to their cautiousness.

"Shall we move?" Ryder asked like he read her mind. Evie stuck a thumb up as her answer. The setup of Potzlan's road network was different from most typical inner core cities. It wasn't a perfect grid structure, instead it was circular. The main streets came out of the center like the spokes of a wheel. There was plenty of space between the connecting streets and maze-like alleys. This place was also dotted with plazas and courtyards, unlike other core cities which had one central plaza. That was located wherever government buildings were built.

This kind of city building was something Evie learned before at Athena. Mostly to study battle tactics though she did learn that these types of cities were popular during the medieval times. Thanks to the way it was built, it left plenty of corner buildings that looked down the many streets with almost no obstructions. It was hell to fight through, there were so many blind spots that one could easily walk into an ambush. The regs already had to learn that the hard way. If she weren't fighting some threat to humanity, this would be a cool place to visit. Apparently, the ones on Earth still stood, so she wanted to see them too one day even if they had to stowaway there.

Ryder led the way down once she had all her stuffed pack up. Evie looked into each room as they descended, some were blown out, exposed to the light of day. Others were untouched, like the residents of this place had never left. The rooms would still be like that if the EEN hadn't had to blow this place sky high. There had to be fifty heavy artillery pieces surrounding this city with near constant bombardments. That was how dug-in the Vekros were. They've killed thousands of them, yet they were easily replaced by more. Evie heard that command couldn't figure out where the Vekros were getting their troops from as they killed fifteen percent more than estimates predicted.

Being at street level made Evie feel small. She had gotten used to looking down on everything. The streets crowded with rubble, personnel, and equipment made her antsy. Things had a tendency to go wrong in the open. Ryder walked down the street confidently with Evie trailing his footsteps. A few support units made their way down the street with them. An APC crawled past, heading in the same direction as Evie and Ryder. That unit should have been here an hour ago to provide the regs with support. Things must be rough out there still if it was taking this long for areas to get reinforced. Commander Kurepina and Commander Horstmann must have their hands full trying to sort out this mess.

A faint whistle caused Evie to look up at the sky. There was nothing there, but the whistle grew louder every second. Her eyes widened as they were out in the open. Evie dropped her rifle, grabbed Ryder's arm and pulled him against a wall. It only took a few seconds after when blasts shook the ground around them. Shells fell down the length of the street and buildings they were conveniently at. It was all over in thirty seconds. Heavy mortars had bombarded the area, rendering this spot of land useless as a place of shelter. The vibration of a truck rolling down the street might even cause one of these buildings to collapse. From what Evie could tell, no one had gotten wounded, well, someone was about to.

"Get off already!" Evie pushed Ryder off to the side and sat up straight.

"Hey! I'm not the one who pulled someone else on top of them in the first place." Ryder countered as he dusted himself off.

"A simple thank you would be nice." Evie crossed her arms and bore a hole through Ryder's gaze.

"Fine. Thank you for saving me." Ryder replied sarcastically, pulling Evie back up on her feet. "Why don't you do this when Lance is around? Stop causing me so much grief."

"Oh, I can't do that to my Lance." Evie said innocently. Ryder opened his mouth to speak, then just shook his head. Evie wondered what he was going to say with that look of pity in eyes. She went around looking for her rifle only to find that it was twisted and bent beyond repair. Thank you, falling rubble. They were going to have to backtrack a mile or two to grab a new one.

"Wow! I can't believe you managed to get your weapon busted up like that." Ryder whistled.

"That just means I can get a better one." Evie shrugged. "I'm aiming for a nice fifty cal.!"

"Maybe aim for something that isn't the size of our captain." Ryder sighed. They found a truck that was heading back to the area command post. There were a lot of wounded that were going back with them. The two operators sat in for the sake of the injured. What Ryder didn't say back there bugged her. He never had problems speaking his mind, it wasn't his style.

"Give it to me straight. What were you going to say back there?" Evie attempted to look Ryder in the eyes, but he averted his own towards the wounded.

"It's not my place to say." Evie wrinkled her nose, disappointed with Ryder's answer. It was his right not to tell her as much as she didn't like it.

"What the hell does that mean anyway?" She pouted, leaning back against her seat.

"You'll figure it out." Ryder replied solemnly. *Maybe he's still down about Lek. Those two were kind of close, I'll miss him too.*

The three Vekros collapsed to the ground. This was the thirtieth building today. Two marines came in after Lance and secured the final room on this floor. There were still two floors before this building was completely secure. This entire operation would go a lot smoother if they had Blackout drones. He'd prefer a solo mission far from any help to this tedious work. It was constantly making sure the marines didn't get themselves killed, and a lot of stairs. Lance was getting annoyed by all the stairs he's had to climb this week. Most of the Vekros were in this part of the city and he hadn't gotten rid of nearly enough for him to feel better.

Progress had been steady, to say the least. With the exception of the inner city, the entirety of the suburbs and the outskirts of the main city were firmly in control of the EEN. Those areas were taken in two days at a high cost. Casualties were above the predicted level by three percent. That was roughly a battalion and a half. The EEN only had so many resources and soldiers it could free up to this city, and starting off that badly wasn't going to give anyone confidence. Lance was trying his best to keep that level from increasing and save the commander's conscience.

"Revenant, sir, this floor is clear." The sergeant reported. His squad was already lining up to ascend to the next level.

"I'll head this group for the next floor as well. Just provide me with cover." Lance took his position and took a few more seconds to make sure the squad was ready. The next two floors were cleared with no problems. The reason being that there were no enemies in the first place. All except two of the floors had Vekros hiding in every corner.

After descending the building, the squad that Lance had been tagging along with was being relieved of their duty for the day. The next squad had that eager look about them. He could admire their spirit for wanting to take the Vekros head on. The same could be said that recklessness could get them killed if they let it get to their heads. Before Lance could join them, he was stopped by a combat medic.

"Masked soldier, hold on, you're bleeding." The medic pointed at Lance's arm. He didn't remember doing that, but it wasn't worth the time to take care of. He faced the green-eyed girl, a strand of brown hair falling from within her helmet; she had the same accent as the intelligence officer.

"It's fine." Lance began to walk away only for the medic to block his path.

"No can do, captain. Let me look at it. It will only take a few minutes." She insisted. Lance sat down on the ground with an annoyed grunt. The medic rolled up his sleeve and there was a good-sized laceration, not that he had dealt with these without first aid. "See, this is enough to warrant my attention."

Lance didn't care enough to look. He knew he'd survive worse wounds. The woman was very attentive and surprisingly gentle. That didn't slow her down, keeping a steady pace dressing the wound. It was enough to interest Lance.

"What unit to you belong to?" Lance asked.

"Squad Three of the Third Platoon of the Eighty-Ninth." The medic replied punctually. "Private Harrison at your service."

"So that's your squad that just went by?"

"Yes, sir. If you want to report me, I can point you to my squad leader." Harrison began to wrap up his upper arm.

"No, need." There was a good stretch of silence between them as the medic continued her work.

"I'd like to thank you for taking care of Second Squad. Especially Mason, he has three kids back home." She expressed. Lance didn't know this Mason and wasn't going to try to remember which one it would have been, accepting the gratitude was fine with him. As she finished bandaging him up, he listened to her talk about the members of her unit, the way she talked about them sounded like his own teammates. Compared to some of the other regs he had to deal with down here, she wasn't hesitant at all about interacting with an operator. Or she could be clueless like Emma was. Whatever the case, Harrison treated him just like any other officer, and soldier at that. *Was this an effect from Commander Kurepina's stance?*

"Alright Private Harrison, the squad is waiting for us." Lance stood up and waited for the combat medic to pack up her supplies and her shotgun. He wasn't entirely sure how she could operate it effectively, so she must have been stronger than looked.

"Yes, sir! I'll follow your lead!" Pvt. Harrison replied with too much enthusiasm. The pair caught up to the squad relatively quickly. Lance took it upon himself to take point. He could react far more quickly than the regs and had the advantage of shot prediction, which the Commander told him that was the science guy was calling it. Truth be told, Lance was tired of seeing soldiers getting killed in this city.

Squad Three, accompanied by Lance entered the Third Ward. A crude wooden sign was there to greet them. *Welcome to Bloody Potzlan.* Those were the words painted in red. The younger representatives of the squad, three of the six, joked about the sign and how the EEN was crushing the Vekros. That cocky attitude was something didn't he didn't like. The damage to this area was catastrophic. Lance had already been here five separate times to rescue trapped teams. This certainly had been a thorn in the side of the EEN's advance. Every time this section was cleared, it was reoccupied within an hour. Ward Three had been bombed and shelled to oblivion. Most of the buildings were standing rubble, and a waiting tomb.

They lined up what might have been a single-story residence at some point. With all the holes and gaps in the structure, who really knew what its purpose used to be. Now it was infested with Vekros. A bigger guy in the squad kicked in a haphazardly placed door, stepping back to let Lance go in first. Four targets were spread throughout the first room. He shot the one with the gun pointed at him, to the one that was swinging its gun towards him, then the other two that had just picked up their weapons. Not giving the others a chance to get ahead of him, Lance rushed further into the decrepit building.

He could "feel" eyes following him through the wall. Lance slid into a room and took out a foot soldier that was immediately to the right of the door. Coming out of the slide, he unsheathed his knife and plunged it into the chest of the other before it could fire. It didn't go down right away, so Lance slashed at its throat, and it dropped like a bag of rocks. Harrison and the others came in not too long after.

"Come on Captain, leave some for us." Some of the grunts complained. They were taking this way too lightly.

"You guys are here to support me. That's it." Lance replied coldly, wiping his knife on the sheath.

"I'm sure our orders were to clear buildings, actually." A soldier spat.

"Shut the hell up Buckley! Do NOT disrespect a superior officer!" The sergeant stepped up and screamed at Buckley's face. "Or do you need to go back to basic!"

"How is that masked freak my superior!" the marine challenged. The sergeant was about to say something before Lance stopped him.

"If you can land a shot on me, I'll leave you alone. But if you miss, then you follow my orders to the letter. Unless you're afraid of the repercussions." Lance taunted. It worked as Buckley's gun was now aimed squarely at him.

"Captain! This isn't a good idea." Harrison tried to get in between them.

"Step aside, I got this." Lance saw a smile crease the sergeant's face like he already knew what was about to happen. Lance observed Buckley's movements closely. The two men stared each other down, then the hairs on Lance's neck and arms raised. He could see the bullet's trajectory. Lance stepped to the side and the bullet zipped past through the wall behind the spot where Lance was. Buckley stood there confused, fearful, and mesmerized all at once.

"Follow orders." Was all Lance said as he walked out.

Things went rather smoothly after that altercation between Lance and Squad Three. It was still building after building against what felt like an inexhaustible enemy. There was no reason why the Vekros should want this place. Which begged the question why they were fighting tooth and nail for it? There were many instances where the Vekros were about to lose. Those times they used long-range bombardment to make the surface of planets uninhabitable. Recently, that wasn't the case. They were preserving the places they captured.

Turning onto yet another boulevard of broken dreams, Lance instantly felt something wrong. He motioned for the squad to hug the walls just in time. Gunfire erupted from several two-story buildings around them. Alone in the middle of the street, all the rounds seemed to be directed at him. Lance dove for cover under the refuge of a semi-collapsed structure. He could hear the report of Squad Three's rifles returning fire on their assailants. Lance crawled through the maze of ruined structures, getting closer to the sound of the Vekros weapons. Coming out from under the rubble, he found himself behind the building that had gunfire inside. The Revenant spent no time getting to work. Diving through the open window, a line of Vekros had their attention out of a series of windows.

He fired into their backs, and the group collapsed in unison. Revenant reloaded the maw as he bounded up the stairs. An enemy fired down the staircase. Making small adjustments to his course and parts of his body, every shot missed by a hair's length. With the maw now reloaded, one shot to the target's helmet was all it took. The gunfire had lessened, meaning the Vekros occupying this building were lying in wait for him. Not wanting to keep both the Vekros and Squad Three waiting, Lance came around the corner and unloaded the magazine down the hall. Three targets fell, and four doors opened to reveal four more targets.

Lance unclipped a grenade and tossed it down the hall before busting through a door. The window had an old clothesline that led to the building across the street. Jumping through the window, Lance grabbed hold of the line as the building shook. The clothesline snapped from the building he had just come from and was swinging down towards the first floor of the target rich building. Gun raised; two three round bursts took care of the enemies in the window. This time the Vekros came to greet him, making the process of killing them that much easier.

Lance switched from the maw to his blade. The foot soldiers took on the challenge and drew similar weapons. They came at him all at once, which under normal circumstances, was a perfect strategy. The reason it wasn't going to work was because they were going up against the Revenant. Lance blocked one attack, using his free hand to bring down its helmet down to his knee. Then a leg sweep brought another down along with a quick slash to its jugular. Coming out of the sweep, Lance plunged the knife under the arm of the third. The first one came back for another strike only for it to take a boot to the helmet. Kicking up a knife of one of the fallen Vekros, Lance threw that at a fourth target. The fifth foot soldier came out with a SMG.

Revenant leapt behind the first Vekros and shoved it into the fifth. Both targets lost their balance and tripped over the other. He switched back to the maw and finished the two Vekros off with a few rounds. Silence filled the space. Compared to the other CQC experiences he had, that one felt tame. Lance exited the building expecting Squad Three to be waiting for him. There was no one there. Heading back to where he had left them, Lance was met with a bloody sight. It was a mix of bodies, both Vekros and marines. The squad was spread out across the street, probably in an effort to save Lance. The combat medic, Harrison, was the lone soldier standing, desperately trying to save the last member of her squad's life.

I wasn't fast enough...

Two shadows moved silently through the streets. Approaching a pair of enemies, the two shadows both put the Vekros into headlocks. After a slight struggle, Misha broke the neck of the foot soldier while Heike just stabbed her's in the back with a knife several times. Misha took it upon himself to drag the bodies to a more discrete location. There was a nice alley that had a torched vehicle, where he threw the bodies behind. When he got back, Heike had already gone into the building. She was up on the eighth floor scoping out their target.

"Careful Adler and Specter. The Vekros have employed the Spectral Windows like on Verdant Prime. We'll cause some ruckus to distract the enemy, let us know when to head to the extraction."

"Copy that, Dove." Heike tapped her ear. She took out her binoculars and intently got to work.

"I've never seen you this motivated for something that had nothing to do with killing." Misha leaned on the opposite side of the window from her. "Nice peeping spot you got here."

"Ugghh! I still don't know why I got paired with him. He never shuts up and I can hear his stupid voice through my music." Heike complained out loud.

"Wow! I'm right here." Misha waved in front of the binoculars.

"That's the point, Verlierer." Heike grumbled.

"Ver- What? That sounds like something cool. Is it a cool nickname?" Misha prodded happily. Heike slowly took the binoculars from her eyes and glared at him, then let out a pained sigh before bringing them back to her face. *Ah, she's no fun.*

Misha reached for his binoculars and brought them to his eyes. There was a section of Potzlan that the Vekros were defending fiercely, like a bear would a cub. Misha and Heike were well within that zone at a very specific location. The Commander had tasked them with finding out what the Vekros were doing, since every scan of this area was jammed before completion. While on the subject of bears, Misha really wanted to pet one. They looked like big playful dogs.

It wasn't one of the flashier missions, but Misha had sure been enjoying all the sneaking around. Even if Heike had almost gotten them caught, more than once, Misha was still able to navigate them to this location. He let the captain deal with most of the enemies they came across. It would have been a lot more entertaining if the little eagle was able to joke around, or not hate him at the very least. They were both looking at the same spot. Heavy defenses wrapped around some kind of open-topped stadium. It looked like all the heavy types of Vekros were located here. Whatever was here, they didn't want the EEN to get. If it was true what Lance did on his way from Raveset, which he had no doubt that it was, then maybe it would take them minutes to kill these Veks.

"We can't see anything from here. Call me crazy, but let's get closer." Misha suggested, taking the binoculars from his face and putting them away.

"That's one thing we can agree on." Heike tucked her binoculars away. "The easiest path will be the entrance on the right since the defenses there are further forward."

"My, you actually observed the area instead of wanting to shoot everything." Misha joked as he rested on arm on her shoulder.

"Shut up! I'm not a hothead. Commander Kurepina and Lance specifically ordered to limit combat." Heike shoved him off her and stomped out of the room. Seriously, out of all the operators, she and Lance were the only ones that couldn't have a little fun.

Misha and Heike crouched low to the ground. It was quite easy to infiltrate thanks to the abundance of cover strewn about. As heavily defended the stadium was, the defenses were spaced out to far apart, leaving gaps and blind spots that the operators could exploit like they were now. The stadium was the most intact building in this entire city, and that wasn't saying much. Many of the support pillars had sustained heavy damage from battles before and the years of neglect. They wandered aimlessly for some time until they entered a long tunnel. There were faded pictures of different sports stars all the way up to the light at the end.

Exiting the tunnel, Misha was overcome by the grandeur of the arena. The seats went all the way up and all the way around. He could only imagine the types of events that went on here, without all the battle damage of course. It would also help if there wasn't a giant hole in the center of the field surrounded by Vekros. Heike pulled him down behind some crates.

"Can I just revel at this sight?" Misha looked at Heike disappointedly. He could tell she was reaching the limit of her patience.

"Focus already! We are going down there." Heike combed the hair from her eyes. "I don't know what crazy shit they're doing, so how about we crash that party."

"Someone's getting unhinged. Let's bury them alive." Misha unholstered his SMG. Heike and Misha vaulted down in unison and opened fire on the unsuspecting enemy. The guns were silenced, but the reverberations caused by the stadium's construction almost nullified that advantage. Lucky for them that Chika's team was causing some chaos a few miles away.

The two operators quickly neutralized the guards above the hole. It wasn't going to take long before an enemy squad would come and investigate. That only meant that Misha and Heike would just have to work a little bit faster. There were some sort of makeshift stairs. They were rather steep, uneven slabs of masonry used from rubble of the city. It went on into the dark underground. Now would have been a good time to throw on some night vision if they bothered to have brought the attachment.

Misha led the way down the dark corridor holding his hand against the wall as a guide. Heike had her hand on his back so they wouldn't be separated. He thought that since they were underground, the wall would be loose dirt, but it wasn't at all. The wall was definitely made of metal or something that was metallic. The floor and the ceiling were probably made of the same material too. There wasn't a single turn, just a straight path that started from the bottom of the stairs. Yet there was a shallow decline as Misha's footsteps felt further away from the one before it. He wasn't sure if his eyes were playing tricks on him as a faint glow had appeared in the darkness. Misha quickened his pace, and little by little, the faint glow became a strong light. He stopped just outside of the darkness and covered his eyes to let them adjust to the new brightness. What he saw was phenomenal compared to the stadium above.

"You see this too, right?" Misha asked in awe. He could feel Heike peer out from behind him.

"Seems like a good place to hide something to me." She responded. They made their way from the cusp of the darkness and into the massive space. In his lack of awareness, Misha lost his footing and was almost looking down into an abyss. Heike pulled him back and he fell against the wall, catching up on his breathing. That was close.

"Would you be more careful! You almost fell to your death!" Heike snapped, sliding off her headphones.

"It's fine, I'm alive." Misha was fine *now*, though he wished that Heike hadn't thrown him against the wall so hard. He rubbed the back of his head where he had hit it. Helmet or not, it still hurt. Getting back up, Misha looked down from the spot he nearly walked off. There was a walkway that led across an open chasm to a giant metal plain that stretched off into the distance. It was like that all the way down as far as he could see. He'd seen pictures of the underground cities of Earth, but this was on an entirely different scale. An army, scratch that, hundreds of armies could hide down here.

"What is this place supposed to be? Have you seen anything like this?" Misha fired off a couple questions as he took out a handheld scanner. The depth indicator had an estimate of seventy kilometers of open space beneath them. He tried it horizontally and it returned with an error message. It couldn't compute the distance, it wasn't determinable.

"How the hell do I know. This is a first to me too." Heike replied in the same awe as he had. "We need to let the Commander know about this... Damn it! There's no signal?!"

"We did go down pretty far." Misha tried to answer as he continued the scans.

"That hasn't stopped it from reaching me when I was inside a mountain." Heike returned. She slid her headphones back on. "This space has that weird staticky feel from the bridge."

"Now that you mention it, yeah. Not as strong, but enough to make me feel like spiders are crawling on me." Misha had flashbacks of the bridge incident. That was a mystery by itself. He stared off into the distant metal plane.

Trying to explore something this huge could take years. That was about the same time the Vekros had to build this giant chamber. Misha though, was not too keen on sticking around here anymore. Exploring and danger may be his forte, except this static feel rubbed him the wrong way. The atmosphere here gave him chills and made him want to turn and run, like he was in more danger than he could handle. A quick look at Heike and he could see a slight, visible shaking. She could feel it too. There was no way they'd ever come back to a place like this.

Chapter 6

Respite; Determination

An endless stream of tapping a pen against the table was the least of the command post's worries. Lera didn't know when she started the tapping, all she knew was that she hadn't stopped doing it for the past few days. Her eyes strained on the holographic map of Potzlan. The inner city was proving more challenging than Command had predicted. All the main streets were either blocked by heavy Vekros equipment or completely impassible due to heavy bombing and bombardments. That left the EEN forces having to snake through the maze-like streets, the threat of ambushes around every corner.

Most of her attention was set on keeping the advance moving forward in tandem with Helen Horstmann's army group. Lera wasn't given much to work with in terms of combat personnel, so she had to be more tactful than usual, even going as far as working with Commander Beverly's unit. She did keep a watchful eye on the operators that were sent out to help all over the city. Every team was on their way back.

The command post was set up on the ground floor of a police station, or what was left of it. Being nearly in the open air and exposed to the elements was a stark contrast to the prefab buildings at the Ceratel Valley. It was hot, with a breeze that only brought hotter air. The command post was also exposed to enemy attack with its close proximity to the fighting, since securing already retaken areas had proving difficult. Taking this risk was fine. It allowed exhausted soldiers to get to a safer area quickly. There were a lot more of them on top of the wounded with each passing day. The nickname for this place fits perfectly.

"Commander, stay focused." A flick to the back of Lera's neck made her jump in surprise. Sgt. Emma Sytnikova stood there full of energy compared to the rest of the staff. Lera eyed her newest subordinate fiercely. "That's more like it!"

"I was perfectly focused until you did that. What do you have to report?" Lera picked her pen back up and went back to the map, or so she thought.

"Operators... something Adler and Specter have found a large cavern under the city. They say its Vekros made and based on past land surveys, it's true that there wasn't any natural cave system under the city. Not that I doubted them." Sytnikova reported. If Lera remembered right, she had sent them to the stadium. The heavy Vekros presence there had prevented them from closing in on it, yet Heike and Misha were able to so easily. Better yet, it led to some sort of discovery.

"Was there anything else?"

"They wanted to tell you more about it in person. I don't know why they were so adamant about that." Emma replied.

"Thank you. Carry on then." Lera couldn't even begin to process the information before Major Rikimaru walked over.

"Lycoris and his team have returned. I hold down the fort for you." The major offered.

"Yes, thank you, Major." Lera set down her pen and went to the border of the safe zone and the battleground. Besides Rene, A'Darrion, and Olivier, another group that was under Horstmann's command was with them. She knew that leader of that group just by looking at him. As heavily bandaged as he was, that man stood taller than the rest of them. He was held in high regard within the Rangers and the military. Blitz Nine.

Outside of the operators, the Rangers were some of the best in the special forces. The man in with her operators was no exception. No one knew his real name or where he came from. Blitz Nine became known after leading the Rangers against a Vekros general. A year later, his team was trapped on a snow-covered mountain after an infiltration gone awry. That group held out for four months, surviving in the wilderness and taking out Vekros before a happenstance EEN operation found them. Since then, Blitz Nine's legend only grew. Lera knew it all too well. That man was one of the reasons she went down this path in the first place. That's when he spotted her and spent no time wasting to come over.

"Well now, I wasn't expecting to see you." Blitz approached and slowly saluted, which she returned. He stepped back with pride in his eyes after the quick embrace.

"It's so good to see you after all of this time." Lera smiled.

"My, you've gotten taller since the last time I saw you. You were about yay big." Blitz raised his hand up to the height she was in middle school. "So, you really did end up in the military, a commissioned officer no less. Boy, don't I feel old."

"I don't remember you being this dramatic. It's only been what, five years?"

"Five years is a long time when you get to be my age. I'm now hearing stories about you, Santo della Vittoria." Blitz emphasized her newfound nickname that she didn't like.

"Eh, can we not mention that. It's about time you got to the infirmary. We can't have you dying on us now." Lera dismissed. She would like to catch up with him a little more if the operators weren't back. The mission comes first, well, they came first.

"I'll do that. See you around, Commander." Blitz waved with his uninjured arm. Lera waved him off and turned to the gate. The three operators were busy sorting things out with the Rangers. While waiting patiently for one set of operators, another pair came walking through, Ryder and Evie. All six operators exchanged surprised greetings, then all came to her at once.

"Don't tell me you guys planned on meeting here at the same time." Lera greeted.

"Heh. wouldn't that be something? No, this is pure coincidence, as you can see, we had to escort the Rangers back." Rene pointed his thumb behind him.

"Yeah! We fought some big machine-like enemy!" Olivier raised his fists and through a few jabs while A'Darrion looked at him with disdain.

"Machine-like?" Lera looked over to Rene for clarification.

"A Quadsteer. A piloted quadruped walker that's a pain to fight." Rene answered. Lera had a vague idea of what it was. She was told to try and avoid fighting those unless supported by heavy armor. It took only the Rangers and Rene's team to take one out.

"Pshh! It might be hard for you! Everything has a weakness that can be exploited by a well-trained eye." Evie chimed in doing a stance a superhero would make.

"Says the one that hides and is skilled at ambushes." Ryder murmured just loud enough for them to hear.

"Hey! Make jokes now, but I'm the one that has your back when I'm hanging off the side of a building, Ryder." Evie stamped her feet on the ground.

"Sure, that's true. That works when your gun didn't get smashed to hell Evie." Ryder and Evie glared at each other. Lera could feel the tension radiate off of them.

It was unlike these two to not get along. Besides Rene and Chika, she thought that Ryder and Evie got along the best. Their usual conversations were so full of banter that it felt like they were a thing too. Ryder always volunteered to go where Evie went, so that's what gave that impression. What happened out there the last couple of days to cause them to behave like this? Could it be the stressful environment?

"Commander! Get back inside! The Vekros are chasing friendlies back to the checkpoint." Rikimaru's voice came to her ear at almost a shout. Then the sound of gunfire was evident only after he had warned her. It indeed sound like Vekros repeating rifles, and the distinct sound of a certain operator's handguns.

"Commander! You should get back!" Rene tried to move her back towards the Ops center. She brushed him off and unholstered her handgun.

"I'm already out here so I'll help. Just get on the armored platforms, take out the closest ones to the checkpoint gate." Rene looked like he was going to be sick for a second before flipping off the safety and taking the operators with him. Lera went right at the entrance, the border between safety and the disputed zone.

Four soldiers rounded the corner of the block with dust springing up behind them. One was being supported by another while the other two provided covering fire. As they got closer, Lera realized that was Lance who was supporting the soldier. She almost ran out there to help but had to stop herself. Getting in a firefight wasn't one of her strong suits and going out there to help would only hinder their progress. Lance would switch his focus from that soldier to her, she knew that. Lera got into a firing stance, aimed at the nearest Vekros that started to come around, and fired. The kickback was stronger than she thought. This was very different from the ones she used to practice with on Earth.

Lera didn't watch the one she shot fall, instead switching to the next closest. Some of the checkpoint defenders created a vanguard around her and coordinated their fire with hers. Another group went out partway to escort the operators back in. The Vekros that were in pursuit must have realized that it was futile to continue the chase and retreated back behind the rubble. Lance handed what was actually a combat medic off to the medical team here. The girl had been shot in the leg and thankfully didn't look serious. Heike and Misha fell against some sandbags, heaving exhaustive breaths while the masked Lance signed something. Lera turned her head just in time to see Rene lift his arms up like an exaggerated shrug.

"Wow Commander! I didn't know you were such a good shot." Lera felt a pat on the back. Chika draped an arm around her shoulder and leaned out from behind her with a smile.

"I'm really not that great. When did your team get her? I didn't see you guys come back." Lera holstered her handgun. Edward and Fio went over to the rest of the operators.

"We took the side entrance, although that meant missing out on the fun over here." Chika looked down in disappointment.

"I don't know if I would call it fun..." Lera heard a rather loud "ah-hem" that caught her attention. Lance didn't have his mask on now and he didn't look particularly happy. *Wait! He doesn't look happy?! It's been a while since I've seen him without a blank expression.*

"Uh-Oh. Looks like your about to hear it now, Commander." Chika expressed her sympathies. So, Lance was unhappy because of her? Lera didn't know what she did wrong to get this reaction, though she was about to find out wasn't she. Lance started walking over to her and she straightened up ready to hear what he had to say. He did something unexpected, taking her by the forearm and walking her behind the generators that powered the command checkpoint. Once they were well behind it, he let go and turned to face her. There was an intensity in his eyes that Lera wasn't used to seeing, the last time being that incident with the Terran Revolutionary Front.

"Uh, Lance- " Lance put a hand up to cut her off. He looked like he was still sorting out what he wanted to say. That after a long uneasy silence, he finally spoke.

"Le- Commander, please don't do something so dangerous again. If you try that again, I'll carry you back to the Ops center myself." Lance glowered. He was mad at her for helping?! That wasn't what she thought he'd get mad over.

"I was out there already, so I didn't see the harm getting involved. Then I saw it was you guys which made me want to make sure you made it safely back." Lera answered. Lance's frown deepened along with his brow. *Why is he getting so worked up about this?*

"It's not your job to put your life on the line for us. Leave the fighting for the ones trained to do so and continue to lead from safety. We're expendable anyway compared to the ones who lead us." Lance rebuked, his voice still level and calm despite the look on his face. The last thing set Lera off.

"Lance! You are not expendable! Not the operators, not the soldiers, not anyone! Don't put me on such a high pedestal when we are all just fighting for the same thing!" Lera snapped at him with gritted teeth. Lance's face softened a bit, a half-smile creased his face. He leaned in closer to her as she went to back away, only to find the generator was behind her. He stopped a few inches shy from her face. The sensation of his breath tickled her neck as her eyes looked into his.

"Kurepina. I chose my words wrong, but I only say this to get you to listen. I really care about you, okay. Is it wrong of me to make sure that you are safe?" Lera felt her face get hot. How was she supposed to answer that? This wasn't a situation she was used to, just like she was being looked up to from the other officers. Lance was just asking as a subordinate would a superior. Except, that didn't line up with what he said. *Does he feel the same way? What was she thinking?! I'm over thinking this, I have to be!*

"I-I want to- " Lance placed a finger over lips to stop her fumbling over her words. This was so unlike her. This was so unlike him! Where'd her confidence go? He was so close he could probably hear her heart pounding. Lera's chest swelled with air and tension. Lance felt closer than he was a moment ago. She closed her eyes with anticipation of what would happen next.

"Am I interrupting?" Lera opened her eyes. Lance was still a mere inches away, his head turned to the right slightly. Lera looked left where Heike was leaning up against the generator. "I can come back. Then our new guest will wonder why I didn't bring our commanding officer with me the first time."

"No. I was just checking to see how exhausted she was. It's not like her to make decisions like the one earlier. Let's go Commander." Lera watched for a second as Lance disappeared behind Heike; she had a cheeky smile on her face then she pushed herself off the generator and followed Lance. She took a couple deep breaths and a few strokes of one of the strands of her hair before going as well. Whatever just happened could be revisited later.

Heike and Lance were talking to a rather tall individual. His features were quite striking, the red hair, ice blue eyes, and slight frame. This soldier was a Veridian like her. Besides her parents, Lera hadn't seen another one ever. Did he come from the planet her parents came from? His accent sounded like that could be the case. Then how did he get off-world? How did he survive the first core world to fall to the Vekros? When she got closer, Lera noticed that his name was covered.

"Commander Kurepina?" The soldier questioned.

"Yes, that's me. How can I help you?" Lera asked in turn.

"This is Lieutenant Kur- "

"There'll be no need for that, sir." The lieutenant interrupted. "I'm just here as a messenger to inform you that you're being relieved. The Eighty-Sixth Army is coming in and taking over for the Fiftieth Combat Corps."

"What? I didn't hear this from Commander Horstmann or Captain James." Lera thought out loud. The operators, specifically Lance, didn't look to happy about it.

"Orders just came in from above. The Fiftieth has seen skyrocketing casualties and EENS Moskva has a 'special' mission that requires its forces back." The lieutenant explained.

"We don't get a rest first?" Lera queried.

"I don't have that information, but I wouldn't expect more than two weeks." Lera bit her lip in frustration. There was no way they could get resupplied and replacements in that amount of time. She also didn't like leaving a fight unfinished. There still was that cavern that Heike and Misha found too.

"I see. Thank you for informing me. We'll move out right away." Lera did a quick salute which the lieutenant responded with one before going back to what looked like soldiers with the emblem of the Eighty-Sixth. It didn't feel right to leave a fight so prematurely. They were so close to finishing it too. What was Command thinking? What's more important than taking back their homes?

Several Hours Later

The sky over the outskirts of Potzlan was as busy as the military port of Yire. All the personnel under Horstmann were being pulled out and switched with General Tybera's Eighty-Sixth. From what Chika had gathered, it was from the high casualties and some other mission that was deemed more important. That was bothersome for a few reasons. Chika wasn't done with this planet, specifically, the large cavern that Heike and Misha found. They way they described it made it turn out to be like some scary beast for which they had to be overreacting. The only part that made it even halfway believable was Heike's wording. If something scared her, then it has to have some truth to it.

Another problem had to do with this next mission. The Moskva was set to travel to a supply station in the Terminicks system and while there, offload the wounded and make minor crew adjustments. In the end, they were about to lose fifteen percent of the Moskva's total crew capacity, not including the ground forces attached to her. For a ship that was only half-manned, fifteen percent is a huge deal. Many features that made the Moskva what it was are going to be greatly reduced in their effectiveness, further relying on the support ships. Therein lies the final problem. Whatever mission the Moskva was set to take part of, she was the sole ship for it, and expected to continue lone wolf for several months after. Chika didn't know much about warships, but as quick and armed the battlecruiser was, that was an awfully big risk to leave your all-singing, all-dancing brand-new battlecruiser to chance.

A crate being dropped snapped Chika out of her thoughts. A'Darrion and Edward were about to get into a scuffle from the looks of it. Rene quickly went over to calm the two down before punches could be thrown. Everyone else wasn't happy leaving here with unfinished business either. Commander Kurepina even went on a rant on the way back to a nearby aerodrome. She was more worried about how demoralized everyone was going to be, not pulling out a victory. At least the laid the groundwork for the next group.

In the end, it might be good for them to leave despite the demoralization. Just watching them carry boxes and crates, Chika could see the tole this battle had on them. It was anything major, but small mistakes were being made way too often recently, and those could mean life or death in a firefight. What's worse is that they continue to happen in something as simple as leaving a combat zone. Chika didn't care if operators weren't meant for long, drawn-out battles. There shouldn't be any excuses for these little hiccups. Teammates shouldn't be at each other's throats, or questioning orders. They had a specific job and they had to do it whether they liked it or not; until things could turn out better for them. She was going to train these idiots hard when they got back on the ship.

"Fio! Evie! That crate goes in that shuttle." Chika pointed at the closest of the four shuttles. The two girls nodded unenthusiastically.

"Everyone, you can take a break after those boxes." Lance exited a large tent with a bunch of mugs.

"Hey! I'm trying to whip them back into shape. Their endurance is terribly lacking." Chika spoke with a rather angry tone. Looks like she needed to take her own advice too.

"I agree with you on that Chika. They on the other hand are tired enough as it is, so training right after this type of battle isn't going to do any good. That said, I'd rather see this fight through than leave when it's almost over." Lance took a long drink from his mug.

"So, your saying you're not tired of this?" Chika tried to get hi to slip up, but he just gave her a look that said he knew what she was up to. The rest of their friends came over and took a cup before flopping down in various spots and positions.

"I hate to say it, not really, but I don't like leaving an unfinished fight either." Heike butt in as she went to change a song. "All of these different orders are just too exhausting to keep up with compared to the actual fight."

"Easy for you to say, the running around all over the place was tiring. All the ambushes and being chased by every Vekros takes it tole. I only wished to return the favor tenfold." Fiorenza complained.

"Hence why I wanted to do some endurance training." Chika did a light facepalm.

"From what the Commander has been saying, we'll get the next couple of weeks to recuperate. It's something we all need right now." Rene took his seat next to Chika. She eased herself into his left arm and laid her head on his shoulder.

"Don't you worry, that'll be more than enough time for that." Chika smiled and kissed him lightly on the cheek.

"Please! Not while the rest of us are here!" Heike glowered.

"Oh, come now, I can't show a little affection but it's alright for you to do more with Lance?" Chika teased. She got the reactions she was hoping for with Lance glaring at her and Evie looking like she was about to melt.

"Hmph! You think you're *so* funny." Heike grumbled, slowly lifting her middle finger like a jack-in-the-box.

"Let's get back on topic please." Ryder jumped in. Heike put her hands down before she could finish making the gesture. Everyone's faces hardened when Ryder began to finish his thought. "Lance and I have discussed this to some degree, but the Vekros change in tactics... is concerning."

"Reviewing their normal battle tactics; The Vekros use overwhelming firepower and numbers to wear away the EEN's forces and achieve victory. Their navy is undoubtedly more powerful overall. When we look at their ground forces, what they lack in comparable equipment is made up by their numbers advantage." Everyone nodded at the key points of Chika's explanation.

"Now looking at them currently, the navy had developed new technology that was overcome by the brilliance of our commander. The Vekros ground troops have expanded into using guerilla tactics and do or die resistance. We know for a fact that they don't change tactics unless something as drastically changed the battle. That raises our key question; why are they changing it up now?"

It wasn't anything anyone here had to answer too based on the downcast faces. If they had put their heads together sooner, they could identify when things began to change. When Chika glanced over at Lance, she could tell what he was thinking. The Vekros clear targeting of the operators, which was at the forefront of her mind as well. She overheard Lance mention something to the commander about it and snippets of what happened at Raveset. During firefights here, she could tell how much fire was directed at them compared to the regs. Then Vekros pursuing operators almost to the safety points. Up until now, they had treated operators as nothing more than regular soldiers.

Chika was still more worried about Lance's encounter with the now dubbed saboteur. He hadn't mentioned anything to them about it yet for one clear reason, fear. The fear of fighting your own comrades, the ones that experienced the same awful things that happened at Athena. Chika didn't know what she would do if it was Rene that was on the other side of the barrel. Would she be strong enough to kill the one she loved the most? That strength would either show itself then or show how cowardly she was not being able to save him.

"I'd dare say that each of you have the correct answer, rather in parts." A voice startled the operators and they looked at the direction it came from. "Although only two out of the three catalysts have been identified."

"Stonewall! What are you doing here?" Chika sat up straight and away from Rene, surprised by the random encounter.

"More importantly, what do you mean by catalysts?" Lance eyed the handler with suspicion.

"Woops! Guess I let that slip." Stonewall murmured, then gave Lance a cheesy smile. "Don't give me that look, it makes me feel like I'm the villain here." Lance responded with an annoyed click of the tongue.

"Come now my subordinates, now's not the time for dilly-dallying. As much as you want to finish the fight here, you're needed for something bigger than this."

"What I hear is that you know something we don't?" Rene questioned.

"Possibly." Stonewall replied with a hint of playfulness. He turned on his heels and went in the direction of one of the waiting shuttles. The operators looked around at each other, and the battle-weary faces slowly changed into determined ones. It was time to get to work.

Lance stared emptily into the locker like the inside would change into a blue ocean, or a purple one. The contents of the locker stayed the same. After they had returned from the surface, the handlers took all of the non-captain operators, with the exceptions of Ryder and A'Darrion. Having nothing better to do, Lance was planning on checking in with the Commander to continue his report and make sure she was feeling well. That was the moment Rene unexpectedly wanted to meet him here of all the places on this ship. Lance preferred not to go to the gym at this time of day.

Most of the regs will be recuperating from the battles on the surface. Lance took off his shirt, something he normally wouldn't do, and placed it in the locker before closing it. He planned on tiring himself out while he was here, maybe it would lead to a good night's rest for once. Delaying the inevitable that was Rene wasn't going to solve anything. Lance thought his attention would be better spent on Chika than him, still Rene kept pulling these strange things out of the blue. The gym on the Moskva was a good-sized one. It had a basketball court, a swimming pool, and a weight room. Rene was waiting in the weight room, already starting to warm up without him. Lance stretched his limbs before stepping on the treadmill. There was no need to ease into it, Lance went into a near sprint.

"Glad you took me up on my offer." Rene said in between breaths.

"Spare your misguided thoughts, I just came here to show you up is all." Lance replied while he continued to run.

"Oh, is that how it's going to be." Rene responded with a smirk. Lance and Rene spent a good amount of time racing each other on the treadmills. Not long after, they went for one of the benches. Rene began putting weights on the barbell while Lance test lifted to determine if they needed more or not. They did by a large enough number a normal person would more than likely tear something trying to lift it.

Rene did the bench press first while Lance spotted for him. There wasn't really a need for it, but now that they entered a friendly competition, it was better to make sure that neither of them overdid it. Lance took the time to observe the other groups in the room. There was still a good number of people here doing their own thing and... Ryder and A'Darrion. Rene put the barbell back in its resting place.

"Good job. You made it through all twenty reps." Lance slowed clapped when Rene finished the reps.

"We're just getting started kid. Come on then, do twenty-five." Rene challenged, tucking in his arms and flapping them like a bird.

"I don't know what your insinuating since it was obvious we'd pass that sooner than later." Lance replied as he got down on the bench and got to work. He performed each rep perfectly and slowed it down for better effect. After he did the twenty-five, he shot Rene a triumphant look. They spent more time working on bench presses, yet the competition was not nearly over. The two went to other parts to workout. Everything from pull-ups to leg presses and everything in between, nothing was left out. Except for the area Ryder and A'Darrion were using. Soon enough, both of them were starting to feel it in their muscles.

"How about we call this one a draw." Rene suggested as he finished his last rep.

"Sure, but I think I won." Lance replied as he continued to work his biceps. Rene wiped his face and hands with a towel, drinking some water after. A commotion in Ryder's direction distracted them for a minute. The man was doing a military press with an impressive amount of weight, more than Lance was willing to take on. Ryder was fairly larger than Lance, so it made sense.

"Go Ryder! You got this man!" A'Darrion encouraged passionately. He got next to Ryder's face and was yelling those encouragements. It had the desired effect and Ryder began to rise up. His face contorted with effort; a vein looked like it could burst with the amount he was putting in. Half yelling, half grunting, Ryder managed to get it to his chest. A second effort got it over his head, throwing it down hard enough the weighed down barbell bounced a couple of times. Everyone that was gathered around cheered and hollered at Ryder's triumph. A'Darrion pushed Ryder in the chest in all the excitement. The regs patted him on the back. Lance couldn't help but smile at what he was seeing.

"That was for you Lek! That was for you!" Ryder shouted, pointing at the ceiling. Lance heard a bittersweet laugh from Rene behind him.

"That's certainly one way to pay tribute to a fallen comrade." Rene wiped the beginnings of tears from his eyes. "Sorry Lance, I couldn't save him."

"It wasn't your fault. If I was there, I would have sensed the bullet and- "

"You can't be everywhere, Lance. Don't even try blaming yourself for something that was well out of your control. Let your older brother shoulder the blame for this one." Lance didn't know how to respond, and Rene went quiet and spaced out. Lance finished the set he was working on before a cough came from the other man.

"Anyways, is there anything you'd like to talk about?" Rene grinned. Lance sat down with a towel over his head. What a turnaround from just a moment ago.

"What are you getting at?" Lance asked before taking a drink from the water bottle.

"Come oonn! What's been going on between you and the Commander of course!" Rene exclaimed. Lance dropped the water bottle, caught off guard by the accusation.

"There isn't anything going on if that's what you mean. What made you think that anyway?" Lance gave Rene a sideways stare.

"My eyes... Chika may have pointed it out first." Rene replied. Lance should have known Chika would put something like this in Rene's head.

"I think she's messing with you."

"Heike saw you awfully close to the Commander earlier today. Coincidence?"

"That girl tells tale tales, and I was checking to see how tired Kurepina was."

"So, there isn't anything going on between you and Kurepina?"

"Nothing."

"Nothing?"

"Mmhmm."

They sat on the bench in silence for a couple of minutes. It did give time for Lance to think. He was sure that he didn't like the Commander in that way. But now that Rene had gotten into his head, Lance was unsure whether he could maintain that stance anymore. He had to admit that some of the things he did were definitely in the realm of strange. Rene suddenly burst into laughter at Lance's expense.

"Looks like it's finally dawning on you. Made up your mind yet?" Rene teased.

"How did you know I was- "

"Thinking about the Commander?" Rene finished his question. "I've known you for a long time, Lance. We are brothers after all. I can see it written on your face, it's about the only time that you don't ever look guarded or weary."

"I... didn't know I did that." Lance whispered.

"Since you're not denying it..."

"I don't know." Lance replied with genuine uncertainty.

"You'll figure it out. A little bit of advice, you better hold on to that." Rene stretched out his arms.

"What do you mean?" Lance asked, taking the towel off his head.

"Hey, I may be your brother, but I can't give you all the answers. Just look deep into yourself and I'm sure the answer will prevent itself." Rene laughed. This brought out a sigh from Lance. *Why are you always so vague?*

"Listen, what if I said I could find where you're from? Perhaps your family?" Rene continued in a more serious tone. Lance looked at him like he was stupid.

"Don't I have my family already?"

"I'm being serious. There's a way I can get this information. I've done it for the others and myself." Rene urged, grabbing Lance by both shoulders. "Don't you wanna know too?"

"Do the others... have something to return to?" Lance wanted to know. Knowing that would mean what Kurepina said was one step closer to actually happening. Rene let go of Lance.

"Yeah, some do. The ones, not just us, that I've helped out. Evie, Ryder, and the other younger operators were all picked up from orphanages. That's why they are more willing to stay with the status quo. Chika has parents back in Osaka on Earth."

"What about you?" Rene smiled painfully at Lance's question.

"Me? I have a mother and a father... And a younger sister. We've met a couple of times now. It was difficult to set those up without PONI catching on. That's why I would disappear on Yire for a day. I've missed so much of my sister's life, yet she's happy to know that I was always there. So, I'm not just fighting for you, Chika, and Heike anymore. I'm fighting for the family I want to return to, with you three in tow of course."

The thought of looking into his past honestly scared Lance. He already blocked out so many things from it, opening another door could make him lose his grip on reality. Seeing Rene's warm smile, speaking so fondly over something that never seemed possible before made Lance want to believe. Then a memory popped into his mind, for only an instant. That familiar face that he could barely make out... And now the sensation of a hand tenderly touching his cheek. Lance instinctively leaned back from it only to realize it wasn't there.

"Just… give me some time to think about it." Lance replied softly.

"I'm here whenever you're ready, little brother." Rene ruffled Lance's hair. Lance let him get away with it this time.

Lance and Rene got up and started putting away the equipment they used. As they were doing that, he caught a person intently watching them from the corner of his eye. Lance stopped next to Rene and pretended to be sorting the dumbbells.

"You see that girl too, right?" Rene whispered.

"Yeah, I was just about to ask you the same thing." Lance replied. Nodding something unsaid, both turned around to confront the individual when they found her right in front of them. It was the intelligence officer that met with them on Yire. Abigail Barrett.

"Something the matter?" Rene asked while exchanging a glance with Lance, who shrugged.

"Nothing at all. One of you looked like they wanted to talk." She cast her eyes on Lance, crossed her arms and leaned up against the wall. "What do you want to know?"

"What were you and the Commander talking about?" Lanced asked almost instantly. Abigail smiled and tucked some of her hair behind her ear.

"Sorry, Revenant. You're not authorized to know that. I can tell you this, if you want to maximize efficiency, think of bending with your legs more." Rene snorted at Abigail's comment.

"Hold on a minute. Couldn't he just ask the Commander himself?" Rene suggested.

"Revenant certainly *could*. At the end of the day, it his in her discretion who she lets in on anything. If she goes against my advice, then that's on her." Abigail's tone betrayed what she was said. Lance had to guess that was the point. He desperately wanted to know what those two were talking about concerning Athena. He also didn't want to cause any trouble for Kurepina. Abigail's eyes flicked behind Lance and Rene.

"I'd like to stay and chat some more since you guys are interesting, but my cue just came to leave. Hooroo!" Abigail waved. Lance and Rene turned to see what caused her abrupt departure.

"Aahh, just the man I wanted to see. Come with me Lance." Noah cocked his head over towards the boxing ring, which was just a bunch of floor mats turned into a makeshift one. Rene patted Lance on the back as he was looking for help to get out of it.

The handler Stonewall was out of his normal military attire. He was now sporting a tank top and shorts, items that were not in his normal wear. Lance watched him tape three circles, one within the other, on the ground. Noah went to set the tape on the ground, then with a flick of his wrist threw it at Lance, which he caught easily with one hand. The smirk on the handler's face made him a twinge uncomfortable.

The rules are simple. We start with the largest circle, and with every five minutes you fail to put me on my back, the circle shrinks. You may use any method you devise to take me down, because you're going to need it." Noah explained and then stepped into the circle.

"I hope you don't regret giving me that privilege." Lance countered as he stepped in to circle as well.

"Please! Let the little sparrow try." Noah taunted, tilting his head up to look down on Lance holding that smirk.

Lance rushed Noah straight away. The best way to beat Stonewall was to take him down in the first few seconds. The longer the fight goes on, the harder it is to take him down. Lance went with a jumping side kick which his opponent slid away from. Lance had to pump on the brakes and just barely stayed within the circle. He tried to take him out right of the gate, this wasn't going to be easy. This man was always good, maybe to good at hand-to-hand combat.

"I see you caught on, leaving the circle is instantaneous death, as I like to call it." Stonewall commented. Lance wasn't happy that he missed his mark the first time, but Noah's avoidance was also a double-edged sword. Knowing he was a great fighter; Lance was also in the same wheelhouse. The two of them were of similar size and the handler beat him out in experience. Lance has seen combat more recently the Stonewall, meaning that the handler had to be rusty. He was confident that he was the better fighter over Noah. Lance went for a grapple that Noah easily spun out of. Noah then tried the same thing on Lance, causing him to jump back out of the way. He had to be careful not to step out when jumping back. The handler so far had been focused on dodging Lance's attacks. Then when he was close enough to the edge, that's when the handler would strike.

Renewing his attacks, Lance stayed on the inside when he launched a strike. Stonewall would feign an opening towards the edge of the circle and Lance ignored it to continue pursuing from the inner side. No matter how hard and fast Lance's attempted strikes were, Noah was just a hair faster. He had no idea why he felt so slow compared to the handler. What he did know was that the smirk Noah had was starting to piss him off. Lance tried to move even quicker, sacrificing the power of his hits would have in order to land them. This time Lance was just barely able to graze his opponent. Otherwise, Noah was still just out of his reach. Going for another side kick, Noah intercepted it with both of his hands.

"First five are up." Stonewall sneered. He pushed Lance backward which caused him to stumble back into the second circle. By now a crowd had formed to watch the two operators take each other on. Revenant versus Stonewall. They looked like they were placing bets on the outcome of the match. When Lance went to attack again, Noah met his strikes. Lance backed off, not expecting the handler to block his attacks, but to continue to avoid them instead. Stonewall's stance had changed from a relaxed posture to one arm extended, one arm kept close with both palms open.

"What's wrong Revenant? Don't tell me you want to quit. I don't allow that, you know." Noah enthused. Lance wiped sweat from his brow.

"You sound rather excited about this." Lance commented.

"How could I not be, I have very good reasons to be." Noah replied.

"Then why don't you attack?" Lance inquired.

"That isn't the name of the game." Noah asserted. *That wasn't much of an answer.*

Following what Stonewall wanted, Lance went back on the offensive. It didn't matter if the circle was smaller, Noah kept on blocking his attacks like he knew they were coming and where. Lance even tried to do fancy footwork and misdirection, Noah's movements were much more fluid and his blocks perfectly timed. The handler pulled off a successful grapple and pinned Lance's arm behind his back, then tossed him into the last circle.

"Last chance, Mister Revenant." Noah announced as he nonchalantly stepped into the circle after Lance. This time there was hardly any room for either person to effectively move. Lance could only take a step or two back before hitting the tape. Noah came after Lance, throwing a series of lightning quick jabs. He tried to keep up the best he could, but with each parry the handler got closer to landing a hit. When he could, Lance made counter attacks of his own. It was back and forth, one attacked, the other defended. Suddenly, Noah pushed into Lance's shoulder and began to drive him back. He dug his feet into the ground; it was barely enough to keep him from going out of bounds, but Stonewall was starting to overpower him. Lance was bending backwards against the surprising strength behind his opponent.

"Is that all you got!" Noah jabbed. Finding new strength, Lance began to push back. Just as Lance was making headway to get back upright, Noah took the pressure away and lunged. Before Lance even realized it, he was up in the air. Stonewall drove down just under Lance's throat and threw him into the ground. Lance coughed uncontrollably as he struggled to get air. Noah stood above him pleased.

"Wondering why I was able to beat you without so much as a sweat? I saved my stamina and watched. You have explosive power for your frame, which I used to my advantage. Knowing you would try and take me down quickly, I let you wear yourself out while minimizing unnecessary movements for myself. All in all, you have improved."

Noah extended a hand after his explanation. Lance took it and was pulled back up to his feet. He was partly beating himself up for not being able to take down Stonewall and for being read so easily. Lance didn't look forward to it that much, but taking on who many people consider the best operator (former) was something that kept him alive.

"I thought I could get back in the end." Lance sighed.

"Quit your sighing, you do that way too much. Like I said, you have improved. Just keep at it. I must be off, or the tow ladies are going to hound me." Noah departed. For one of the few times, Lance was exhausted after a fight. Challenging Rene right before another factor. The crowd that had come to watch had mostly dispersed. A group of marines exchanged glances and whispered to each other. Then they came to him.

"Hey, we watched your fight. Mind showing us a few of those moves? We would really appreciate it." One of them requested. As tired as Lance was, maybe he could spare some time. Was this also the Commander's doing?

Ever since the start of the Kanto-IV operation, Lera had been working non-stop. There hadn't been much time to spend with the operators except for those fleeting moments on the surface. In a flash, two incidents popped into her mind. The one on the roof and the one behind the generator. She wasn't quite sure of what to make of those two things. It's not like she had the time to dwell on them right now anyway. Maybe it was something good, maybe she was overreacting and overthinking. Then the fighting in Potzlan was a nightmare.

Naturally, her ability to read the frontline wasn't much help within the confines of the city. It gave her a shudder thinking what kind of battle it would have been if it occurred in a super metropolis like New York City or Boston. While she stayed behind couped up in a command center, Lera had to run her operators ragged. It pained her not to be there with them as they performed heroics time and time again. Lera had to separate them to cover more ground and it was still constant missions. It wasn't fair to them how hard they worked only to not finish fighting either. There was one thing, it was going to take some time to put it into motion though. Right now, she had to clean up after a certain man's mess, a welcome one at the very least.

"Private Caitlin Harrison, combat medic. Your unit had seen some pretty nasty battles. I've read up on your portfolio and it makes sense why Captain Field sent me the letter of recommendation. How's your injury?" Lera complimented the girl who shuffled nervously in her seat. It was mostly for surviving for as long as she had, considering the mess Potzlan was.

"Tha-Thank you, Commander! I'm feeling a lot better now." Caitlin stuttered.

"Calm down." Lera laughed. "I'm fine with you if the captain believes in your abilities. On a more serious note, you do know what they are? It won't be a problem, will it?"

"Yes. I've heard stories about them. When I saw the mask, I had no doubt. I owe the captain for saving me from my own selfishness." Caitlin replied. Sadness shot through the girl's eyes. Lance was with her squad when that tragedy took place, it might take Caitlin a long time to work through that.

"I'll allow your transfer, welcome to the team. You're going to be joining Cerberus Squad as the first non-operator." Lera directed the next part to her "assistant" Emma Sytnikova. "Can you take Harrison to her new quarters, show her around, and take a break if you want."

"Yes, Commander! So, Caitlin, was it? Where are you from?"

"I'm from Ientoran." Their voices faded further away. It may not seem like it sometimes, Lera was happy about the two recent acquisitions. Sytnikova proved herself capable being able to keep up with all of the reports and orders and keeping Lera informed. Having a dedicated medic accompanying the operators was another nice luxury. She was confident Caitlin would be able to acclimate to the pace the operators worked at. A few among them would help her with that.

It was the perfect time for Lera to stretch her legs and check on the different sections of the ship. It was usual for Captain James to join her in some of the routine checks, but he was taking it easy after suffering a migraine. Still, it looked like she wasn't going to have much downtime. What she'd give up to spend some time with Auri, it's been too long since they had a good chat.

Her first stop took her all the way to the rear of the Moskva. She wanted to make sure that the engines and reactor were in working order before they performed a test. In the major operation before this one, the railgun caused the reactor to exceed a safe output and overloaded a mechanism near the gun. Thanks to Oskar and the engineering crew, some minor tweaks were made and that seemed to fix the problem. Lera was here to check for any unforeseen problems after firing the railgun multiple guns. The lead engineer, Corey Baxter, had the crew running on all cylinders. Maybe it was because she was taking time to inspect the ship before departure, or maybe it was the scheduled reactor test, but she left impressed. Baxter went on about power readings and the workings of the Aurelet crystal reactor. Most of it was beyond Lera's comprehension, so she followed along as best she could.

The next spot she wanted to look at was the medical wing. In part from the number of casualties experienced in the Battle of Potzlan. The severely wounded already had been transferred to the hospital ship, Sanctuary. The lesser injuries were kept here in the heart of the Moskva. The problem was how to circumvent the dwindling medical supplies. It would require either resupplying at Yire or requisition from another ship. Before she left, Lera wanted to visit a special patient.

"Knock, knock." Lera called.

"Commander Lera! You came to visit!" Oliviana chimed. For being hooked up to a machine, she sure had plenty of energy.

"I got lucky today. Are you listening to Doctor Edwards?"

"Yeah. Lance said if I was good that he'd bring me another book." The little girl beamed. "Where is he?"

"I'm not sure. I think he had some work that he had to finish on." Lera replied. Lance never knew when to take a break, so that guess couldn't be too far off.

"Aaww. I haven't seen you guys for a long time." Oliviana's head drooped. It must be hard for a girl that young to be trapped in one room all the time. It was only on the good days that she was allowed out of this space. Oliviana has touched the planet's surface for over a year now. It really was unfair.

"That's just part of our job. A lot of people are counting on us, including your dad."

"I wish I could help too." The girl pouted.

"Oliviana, you already are by training really hard and taking your medicine." Lera pointed at the drip bag. "I gotta go, but I'll make sure to drag along Mister No-Show next time."

"Okay! Then you can watch me beat him!" Oliviana declared, almost ripping the tubing from her arms to the dismay of Doctor Ortiz when she jumped to her feet.

"I'm sure you will." Lera agreed.

Lera finished up a couple of other routine check-ins and finally made it back to her room. She tossed her cap on her desk then sank into the unsinkable mattress. No one would mind if she just disappeared for an hour or two, would they?

"It's really not nice to ignore people." Abigail's voice interrupted her plan.

"How'd you even get in?" Lera talked into her pillow.

"I'd tell you, but we got work to do." Abigail responded and pulled Lera into a seated position.

"I know I agreed to this. Can't we do it some other time though. I just got back from Kanto a few hours ago." Lera complained. Abigail handed Lera her screen device.

"You know as well as I how important we do this. To get started, why don't you tell me what you received."

"Don't you already know what is in it?" Lera stretched herself out and got more comfortable.

"More or less. We still need to organize everything still." Barrett responded.

"What were you doing for a month?" Lera mumbled before going through the email. "Not many of the files had any substance. Most contained relatively minor things like business transactions and supply requisitions."

"I know what to do with those. As long as PONI isn't involved, I should be able to trace each one of those."

"The first thing that caught my attention was the file on the head of the project. This one here. Doctor Marilyn Farver. She's pretty impressive, two Ph. Ds, two Masters, lead researcher in multiple extraterrestrial biology projects and human biology. Compared to me, is there anything she can't do!"

As Lera reread the file, the dumber she felt. This woman accomplished so much in fields she never heard of let alone understand. A conversation with this person was bound to be insightful if not confusing. Maybe she could be an ally within the project.

"Is it possible she's the one that sent this?" Lera asked.

"Hmm. It's possible, but more on the unlikely side. A whistleblower tends not to implicate themselves. Though whoever this is, is really committing treason." Abigail answered. "I do want to skip to the point. Where the operators are from and how they become operators." Lera also was wondering about that. None of her operators ever mentioned anything about their training. The only thing she got was that they were all orphans.

"I got this from my team. They are all orphans that were picked up by Athena Corps." Lera informed.

"I see, so that's what they went with. I have a little more insight. While you were away, I did some homework. Let me ask. Where do you think the operators came from before Athena?" Abigail looked like she was trying not to blurt out a secret.

"I'd assume mostly from the colonies where EEN oversight is lax to say the least." Lera guessed.

"You're partly right, though you have to remember that ninety percent of the colonies and fifteen percent of the core worlds were taken within ten years of the war. Some do hail from the colonies, but most come from Earth."

"How do you know?" Lera questioned.

"It's relatively simple. They still have their birth names, and thanks to you, they throw them around like they are one of us. Don't give me that look, it's just for perspective. Anyway, I connected back to the servers on Earth and searched up their names. Many were in the system and were orphans like we established."

"It sounds like you're alluding to something." Lera commented.

"Indeed. What if I told you that not all of them are orphans." Abigail dropped the bombshell. This made Lera shoot up at attention. This raised so many questions and she didn't know where to start.

"Using the same process as before, I couldn't find anything on a good portion of the operators I looked into. It was like they never existed until their filing into the EEN database. Thanks to the extensive internet system back home, nothing is truly lost. Good thing for us those geniuses in Athena didn't think to scrub the servers clean of any information of their operators' former lives."

Abigail took a pause to drink some water. Lera was close to wanting to rock in place in anticipation. If she asked her operators, would they be willing to tell the truth now? Or did she still have to work more and earn their trust? Who would she ask if she did? Chika or Rene might answer. Would Lance? Abigail cleared her throat.

"What I found out was that there was a rash of kidnappings and missing child reports." Abigail finished.

"Meaning that if word got out about this project is a borderline crime ring, we could shut them down." Lera inferred.

"We don't have the proof as of yet, but pairing the reports along with any more information you can milk from your new info broker. It certainly is possible to form a special committee to investigate the upper echelons of the EEN along with Athena Corps." Abigail replied. Lera and Abigail went through some of the other things that were sent in the email. She was pleasantly surprised to learn how much Abigail had prepared for this meeting and all the connections she was making. Lera honestly felt bad for not being able to provide more for this meeting. But she was now distracted, not knowing as much about her operators and Lance as much as she wanted to.

"Oh, before I leave, I was able to get those pictures for the operator's files." Abigail pulled out her phone and started scrolling through. The pictures weren't really professional as the first few operators (Evie, Chika, and Fiorenza) were doing poses. Lera went to have a drink of water and the next picture made her spit it out.

"Wh- What is this!" Lera stammered. Barrett flipped the phone around to see what picture it was.

"Oh. That's just Captain Field."

"Yeah! I can see that! Why is he shirtless?" Lera didn't know if she was embarrassed for Lance, or for her own reaction.

"I was looking for him for so long, so when I happened upon him, I just took the picture." Abigail went to change the picture when Lera swiped her phone away.

"Give me that. And… There. I deleted the picture. Please take a more appropriate one this time." Lera reprimanded.

"Mmhmm. Why'd you send the picture to yourself?" Abigail grinned.

"Shut up!" Lera tossed a pillow at her. "I just have a personal issue I'm trying to work out!"

"If that's all… I'll be in touch. Hooroo!" Abigail waved.

Hooroo?

Lera did have some sort of a plan for that picture. She palmed the locket she received from Lance. It was still empty inside. For a while, Lera couldn't make up her mind about who would go inside the locket. The months went by and her and Lance were constantly working together. Sometime then maybe, she thought it to be alright if it was him. Lera patted her face to get that weird feeling out, it was time to get back to work.

Intermission IV

Ghosts I

The targeting indicator flashed green and red. It was almost locked on to the gun emplacement. The crew manning that gun was very efficient, firing a round every six seconds. The force of the blast caused Lance to jostle around and have to reacquire his target. The captain helped hold the lightweight launch system steady. Lance wasn't quite strong enough to hold it by himself.

"The other two have you covered. Just focus 212." Iron Hand gritted. Lance calmed his breathing and tried to focus. Soon enough, the indicator turned green. "Backblast!"

Lance pulled the trigger and a rocket shot out of the tube. It arced towards the gun emplacement and struck just behind the gun mount. A spectacular explosion occurred as ammunition placed nearby ignited. The first obstacle has been taken care of.

"Let's move! Don't give them a chance to counterattack!" Iron Hand bellowed.

Iron Hand rushed ahead of Lance, followed by his other two teammates. Lance was quite smaller than those three so it was all he could manage to keep. When he started doing these missions, he had no idea how hard these guys went. Typhoon certainly knew how to have fun. The squad advanced under heavy fire, that was fine for them. Captain Iron Hand's motto was *Hail of bullets, cheatin' death.* The head of the formation was always the captain. No matter what the fight was with or what location it was, Iron Hand could be found leading the charge. Lance was placed in the rear of their formation. It was mostly because he was still new to this, but also for his spatial awareness and his quick reactions.

The Veks rushing to their defenses were cut down before they could cause any trouble. The squad had broken through the perimeter defenses of the former EEN military complex. Typhoon was tasked with retaking this base, relatively simple and straightforward. The above ground portion of the base were eight bunkers that were all interconnected. The main complex was built underground. Gambler and Shrapnel picked off targets on the right and left flanks. Iron Hand wrenched open the bunker door the Vekros were trying to close and mowed down the group. He waited for Lance and the other two to catch up.

"212, with me in this bunker. Gambler. Shrapnel. Go to clear the rest of the top bunkers and meet us down. Let's see if you can earn that nickname 212." Iron Hand charged right into the bunker. All Lance could do was try and keep up with the guy.

The captain busted through another doorway and took down the Vekros machine guns. Lance came in a second too late and out of breath. Iron Hand prodded the bodies with his boot, looking out through the opening that overlooked the field. Lance could see the path Typhoon took to get here. The thickets provided excellent concealment; it had allowed them to get the first shots off at the defenders.

"I'll give you a minute, but we have to keep moving." Iron Hand told Lance.

"Yes, sir." Lance leaned forward on his arms to stare at the surrounding scenery some more. It was mostly trees beyond the fields, then more fields behind those trees, like the pattern of his camo. He heard a rustle behind him and found the captain smoking a cigarette. Lance remembered a few of the guards at Athena used those too, and he began to wonder what they were like if people seemed to be so fond of them.

"Don't even think about it little man." Iron Hand warned with a hard stare. He exhaled a plume of smoke. "This is just a habit from before, trust me, it's not something you want to try."

"Oh." After exactly sixty seconds, the captain flicked the cigarette to the ground, and they descended a ladder. They were officially in the main complex of the base. At the time this place was created, it was used as a nuclear weapons launch site. It never had the chance to use them. A gaping hole was left in the side of the hill where the missile would have been located. A Vekros destroyer was the likely culprit for that.

The captain slowed his pace somewhat. They could stumble right into any number of Vekros if they didn't proceed cautiously. Lance would have preferred to move a little slower, like how Rene would guide them through the trap maze. Iron Hand was not the guy to take his time. He wasn't exactly being stealthy either, his gun-mounted flashlight on full blast. Lance kept his off since the captain was providing more than enough illumination.

The halls echoed their footsteps. Lance was sure he could hear gunfire, but from where could not be determined. Iron Hand hugged the wall as the two came up to an area that split three ways. A Vekros soldier came around and Iron Hand quickly broke its neck. The captain glanced down the opposite hall to see two more flashlights. It was Gambler and Shrapnel.

"Glad to see you two boys make it down. I was going to bust your asses if you couldn't handle a few Veks." Iron Hand asserted.

"Yo boss, thirty ain't nowhere near enough dudes. Shrapnel got ahead of me by four." Gambler complained. Gambler and Shrapnel had a little competition, the score between them was well into the thousands. How they remember the numbers, Lance didn't know.

"Alright Forge, tell us what you got."

"With pleasure Iron Hand. There're two more levels besides the one you're on. The bottom floor should have a heavy hitter. A magus. Keep your guard up Typhoon."

"Haha! Let's go kill us a magus!" Iron Hand roared.

A magus was a special type of Vekros. For reasons unknown, they were able to float a foot or two off the ground. Whenever one was around, the Vekros around them became tougher enemies to deal with. It was almost like they became possessed. The crutch of that was if the magus was taken out, so too would the other Vekros units.

In Typhoon squad fashion, they group rushed down the descending hallways. It wasn't just to complete the mission. In fact, the captain would want the mission to go on forever. That was just the type of guy he was, never taking the time to enjoy the moment. It was so unlike how Rene went about things. The squad spread out as best they could in the corridor. The entrance to the "courtyard", a parade ground like area, loomed in front of them. Iron Hand used slightly different hand motions to give out orders. Thanks to all the drills he'd done, Lance understood what was expected of him. The captain counted down from three.

Once the last finger went down, the squad sprang into action. Shrapnel went left, Lance went right, and Iron Hand and Gambler went straight ahead. From the glance Lance took, there were about a hundred enemies below them. The magus was at the center of the horde of Vekros, which was an accurate description thanks to the unnatural way the foot soldiers acted. If he got the shot he needed, that thing would die, unless it had that ability...

Lance couldn't hear his own breathing from all the gunfire and the sound of bullets ricocheting. He began to fire on the move, taking down a few Vekros foot soldiers. It wasn't easy and many of his shots missed their mark. Real combat was nothing like the training, even if the Athena guys were crazy. His assault rifle wasn't well suited for this, but getting a headshot from this distance was still in the cards. Shrapnel was doing the same thing on the other side. The only difference was that he was there to distract and give Lance an opening. Iron Hand and Gambler just charged because they wanted to fight something.

He got to the spot that he was designated. Lance steadied the rifle against a pillar. If he didn't, his shaking would cause the bullet trajectory to be off. The magus sat unmoving, then its head snapped towards Lance. That caused Lance to fire and miss wide. His position had gotten exposed. Trying to fire again would be useless. Lance bolted towards the magus as his position came under fire. At least closing in made it easier to kill the small fry. He zigzagged in between portions of cover and groups of foot soldiers. The erratic nature of his movements caused some friendly fire between the Vekros. Lance stopped behind a low wall.

It wouldn't provide cover for very long. The magus was sure to have a sizable group converging at his location. Lance had to believe that Iron Hand and company was a big enough distraction. Which way should Lance roll out from? Did the magus expect him to come from the left or the right? It was a fifty-fifty shot. Unless there was a way to increase those odds. Lance tossed his rifle to the right as he rolled left. While doing so, Lance pulled his knife from its sheath. The ploy worked, the foot soldiers had advanced towards his abandoned weapon, leaving a clear shot to the magus. Lance moved so fast it felt like he floated that distance.

The magus noticed Lance rushing at it. It tried to move, but it was too late. Sliding beneath the space between the Vekros and the ground, Lance slashed down its leg. The magus crashed to the floor writhing in pain. He brought the knife around and smashed it against the Vekros helmet. The magus went limp, then the clattering and thudding of armored bodies filled the courtyard.

Through all that sound the footsteps of his captain reached his ear. Iron Hand offered his hand, which Lance took, and pulled him back to his feet. Lance's head was still spinning. Rene had always told him to play it safe and smart. What he did just now was not that, but this was a hell of a lot more fun. Checking himself over, he was perfectly fine besides all the dirt. Lance didn't totally understand, but somehow, he could just avoid getting hit. Maybe it will be something he'll play around with more.

"Forge, target has been neutralized."

Forge had no more orders for Typhoon squad for the day. Instead of leaving the shelter provided by the bunkers, Iron Hand used the easternmost bunker as their rest stop. The three members of Lance's squad were talking and laughing away inside while he laid on top of the structure. Watching the stars, he wondered how the rest of his family was doing. *Hopefully better than how I am.*

This was the end of mission two-seventy-three. That was another thing the Iron Hand and Typhoon were known for. Never taking a meaningful break. Besides the ones in between missions, like this one, Typhoon was always fighting somewhere. The good thing that came out of this is that Lance felt like he learned a lot. Shuffling behind him caused Lance to look at the source. Iron Hand climbed up, sat next to him, and lit another cigarette. For a while, it was just silence between the operators. The stars watched far above; each one as bright as his future now that he escaped Athena.

"Do you know why you missed that shot?" Iron Hand exhaled smoke.

"Because I got spotted." Lance sat up and answered.

"That's part of it. You got rattled when that magus spotted you. Sure, it was unexpected, but mistakes like that could be costly. Make sure to keep it cool and next time, that miss will become a hit."

"I won't let you down, sir." Lance replied. Iron Hand slapped his back in approval. Lance tapped his foot against the ground, wanting to say something, though not sure how.

"Spill it kid. You look like you want to piss." Iron Hand coerced.

"Umm... I was... I was wondering if there's a way to find out if my family is doing well. Or if I can see them." Lance stammered. The captain took a long drawl from his cigarette.

"Listen here kid. You're gonna have to not think about them. I'm not saying that it's impossible, but they could be clear across the galaxy for all we know. They might be gone, but you gained new family in us... and every single operator now is part of your family. We fight with each other. We eat with each other. We die for each other."

The captain got really quiet after saying those words. Lance felt depressed after hearing that. That the chance to see Rene, Chika, and Heike were almost zero. What he would give right now to just hear their voices. Rene said he would be alright, but every day that he didn't have them around him hurt more and more.

"Come now, the other two are gonna eat the entire rations if we don't get down there." Iron Hand lifted Lance to his feet with one hand.

"Sir."

Typhoon shared a hard-earned meal. It wasn't anything special. In fact, Lance wasn't even sure what it was. All he knew was that it was chock full of things that a soldier needed to stay in the field. Protein, vitamins, and everything in between. The taste was not all that great, if downright awful. It was still preferable to starving. Lance watched as Iron Hand, Gambler, and Shrapnel played cards. The three glared at each other with serious looking expressions, taking the time to glance at their cards every now and then. Lance didn't understand the game. The goal was to get rid of the cards, and they did that... sometimes. It just took them forever to ever get to that point. They just seemed to keep drawing cards. Gambler drew, then Iron Hand, then Shrapnel.

"All in." Iron Hand threw down two packs of cigarettes. Shrapnel looked over his hand nervously.

"Damn it. I'm out." Shrapnel tossed his cards down.

"I won't back down. Hit it captain. Uhh? Captain?" Gambler waved a hand in front of Iron Hand. The captain nodded slowly, then looked at his subordinates with a grin.

"Tomorrow boys, we got a hell of a mission. We're going to take out that big anti-battleship gun." The three exchanged fist bumps. Lance wasn't sure that he could fully get behind that attitude of theirs. Though, it was still infectious enough that even he felt a little excited instead of fear. After this mission, Lance was going to make it a goal to better understand his family.

Chapter 7

Thousand

Kevin always liked their bedroom dark; it was so much more relaxing that way. Jennifer had been trying to convince him to paint the bedroom a different color, something lighter like sea blue. There were plenty of reasons why he was against it, it was too damn bright for his liking. Speaking of his wife, she was already up and about getting things ready before work. Kevin looked at his phone, it read 7:29. He got up and changed into his uniform, gathering the things he would need for the day.

"Daddy! Your food is right here!" Isabell squealed. That bundle of energy was already ready for school with no problems today.

"Hey pumpkin." Kevin kissed her forehead. "Are you happy school is finally back?"

"Yeah! I'm a fifth grader this year." Isabell replied excitedly.

"That means we'll go somewhere special for dinner to celebrate your first day in fifth grade tonight. Jen, thanks for breakfast, but I'm taking it to go." Kevin put the contents of the plate in a plastic container.

"Okay. Remember to get home earlier if we plan on eating out." Jen reminded. "Have a good day at work, I love you."

"Love you too, dear."

The drive to EEN command was roughly forty-five minutes. An hour if he went and picked up coffee first. It wouldn't hurt if traffic was a little lighter. That wasn't likely to happen since every vehicle that this way was going to the same destination. Kevin got to work once he reached his office. It felt like he had a thousand emails to sort through, then there were the files and documents on top of that. Not to mention he had to periodically visit different offices and departments along with attending meetings throughout the day. Just because he was able to go home in the evening didn't mean the war was put on hold.

Transitioning from deployment to office work was a whole different beast. Some things were able to stay the same, but even more of it was foreign. It was tough, and he wasn't sure that he could pull through. The months wore on, and with the help of his wife, Kevin settled into things bit by bit. He even got a therapist to help him sort out the things he experienced. That was a work in progress. From time to time, his thoughts did bring him back to the ones he had left behind. At least Kevin could help from here, that's what Valeriya wanted. Coincidentally, a request was put through to him from her. It certainly was an interesting thing to send. She probably wanted to guarantee that it would happen. Kevin was sure he could convince some people to allow it. His office door opened revealing his partner in crime, which she hated that phrasing, but Kevin thought it was funny considering her background. Valery Hepburn.

Valery is another person who has been influenced by the brilliance of Valeriya. Apparently, they worked together on the same mission, though she never talked about it much. She did reveal that she was working for PONI along with this post. Kevin had his misgivings at first, anyone from PONI he really didn't want to associate with. Time went by and he quickly realized she was someone he could trust. Besides that, Valery had been wearing a giant walking boot for as long as he'd known her. Kevin made the mistake of asking about it, for which she gave him a look and said, "I think I'm going to throw up." He knew better than to pry open old wounds, knowing he also carried his fair share. When it came down to it, her help was invaluable, and she had a way of persuading others to their cause.

"Good morning, Valery, how's the commute?" Kevin began. The PONI operative put down a stack of mail.

"Same as usual. My sister started her senior year of high school today, so there's that bit of news. By the way, the Chief wants you in his office in five." She informed him after taking a seat at her desk.

"Thanks for the info. I guess I'll be back in a bit, and I want to hear a little more about your sister." Valery smiled slightly as Kevin left the room. When the Chief called, it was best not to keep him waiting. Not that Freeman cared, but he didn't want to keep his boss waiting. Kevin knocked before entering the Chief's office. He found the man standing in front of a great board, there were many words written on it, almost all in shorthand that only that Chief Freeman could read. The Chief welcomed him in and motioned for him to take a seat.

"I want to start off this meeting by formally welcoming you to E-Command. My time has been spent coordinating the four battlefronts, not leaving me with enough time to welcome you properly. The Chief grabbed two glasses and poured scotch in each one. Then he pushed one of the glasses towards Kevin while he took the other.

"I was eager to get to work too, so I'll take the blame for that." Kevin took the glass and took a sip. He was impressed with how smooth it was, comparatively different from his go to, beer.

"I've recently come to know that you are acquainted with a certain commander by the name of Valeriya Kurepina." Freeman gave his full attention to Kevin.

"Umm. I mean, yes, sir." Kevin didn't know why those eyes constricted his breathing. There wasn't any need to be nervous. It was just unusual to be around a man so well revered. "Commander Kurepina and I fought together on Verdant Prime. She has a knack for getting under the Vekros skin and confusing them. I can personally vouch for her if she has done anything."

"It's alright son. It does help to see yet another believes in her ability to lead." Amante laughed. "A lot of things about her, or from her appear on my desk. Just from her efforts from two campaigns she participated in alone is grounds for a promotion."

"That doesn't surprise me in the slightest, sir." Kevin smiled.

"What I really wanted to talk to you about is all thanks to Commander Kurepina's efforts. She has demonstrated the value of using the operators as their own cohesive force. A powerful battalion sized force could easily take a planet with little support. That idea is gaining traction within upper levels of command here. Of course, their core value in infiltration won't be thrown to the wayside. I would like you to formulate that force for its eventual implementation." The Chief offered.

"Yes, of course, sir. I won't let you down!" Kevin exclaimed. This was the perfect project to get. The Chief was handing him free reign to decide how to best make a functional force of operators. Obviously, Kevin had a slightly different idea in mind, but he could make the both of them work.

"Good. You're dismissed." This was Kevin's first big assignment, or second if he counted Valeriya's request. It was going to be interesting trying to create this hybrid force. There was a lot of information he was going to have to pour over, like future operators. As a military officer, it would be nice to see them in action before making a final decision. Thanks to how every aspect of the Athena Project was kept behind red tape, it wasn't likely that he'd be able to do more than coordinate in that respect.

He knew that the core group that was aboard the Moskva could not be separated. They would serve perfectly as the glue that would keep this operator force together. Those three squads were also going to be key in integrating the new operators into the EEN and into mostly normal lives if Kevin had his way. The problem was getting them on the Moskva in the first place. He hadn't stepped foot on the battlecruiser since he left, but it had to be fully staffed by now. No way the newest EEN ship wouldn't be. Maybe it would be possible to get other veteran squads into the force. It wasn't like he wanted to take away talent, it just made more sense having battle-hardened soldiers who already knew the system. It simply was more efficient. Kevin was going to have to see the operator candidates then make his decision. Valery might have some insights with her being in PONI and all.

Amante waited for Kevin Garcia to leave the room, putting the man's empty glass on a tray. He reached over to the phone that was lying on his desk. It had been sitting there with another person on the line. When his old friend reached out to him, Amante wasn't sure how to react to it. Going along with this might reveal some answers and perhaps a new path to pursue, or it was all wishful thinking.

"Did you catch all of that director?" Amante asked after pressing unmute.

"I didn't think you'd go that route." Adolf responded perplexed.

"The instructions you gave me were insightful. I just felt like going off script. There is a strong argument for the way I went with this. What I want to understand is all your misgivings surrounding Valeriya." Amante poured himself another drink.

"Only a hunch my dear friend." The PONI director replied curtly.

"Well, I hope you know she is immensely popular right now. She's already being called a hero of humanity. If you find anything damaging, it must go through me first. The morale of our troops outweighs any precedence you have. We are on the cusp of routing the Vekros from the core worlds." A scoff could faintly be heard on the other end of the line.

"We've been close for years, but I guess I'll have to trust you on this one." The director said dismissively.

"What do plan to do next, Director?" Amante probed.

"There's a small, insignificant blemish that I need to take care of. Nothing that requires your attention."

"Hmm. Talk to you later Adolf. Don't work too hard." Amante ended the call. That man was planning something. Ever since the incident with the TRF, Adolf had his hands full. PONI and the EEN had been covering it up, only that the TRF was growing both in size and boldness. It was only a matter of time before they struck a military target or someone really high up politician. It didn't help that some of the TRF leadership were former military officers. Amante had been running the same system ever since he took charge. That was something they were going to have to change before the TRF could strike. He couldn't have them infiltrating the upper echelons of the EEN.

Then there was the enigma called Valeriya. Amante wasn't going to deny her talents and wished for her success. For him, it was to early to say whether she was a tactical genius or just extremely lucky. Preferably, having both qualities made for great generals with a little bit of crazy mixed in. She didn't have that last part. That said, the way she brought out the best in the operators is unparalleled. Not him nor the handlers were able to achieve that feat as successfully as her. The weapons themselves have more than proven their worth. Somehow, this girl wet behind the ears unlocked the hidden potential inside the operators. The EEN tried a similar experiment in the past. Simply put, it failed miserably. What was different now than the first time? Something that would show itself with time. *Show me more, Valeriya. Show me how capable you can become.*

Lance stared at the darkened ceiling without a shred of fatigue. It had been only a couple of hours since the general lights out time. A feature that the ships had was dimming or increasing light to simulate the diurnal cycle of a planet. This in turn stimulates circadian rhythm that most everyone has. For Lance... it wasn't that simple. Nights were what he dreaded. His comrades wouldn't let him rest. They followed him wherever he went. He wouldn't get any rest until he killed every last Vekros that took them from him. Lance couldn't help but reach for the tablet that lay beside him. His team had accidentally stumbled into the world of "social media". Well, that's what Chika called it. They themselves didn't have the authorization to actively participate in what was on it, but they could look through it. It really was of no interest to Lance. That didn't stop the others from showing him useless things.

Countless minutes of looking at mail made him realize this wasn't going to make him tired enough to sleep either. Lance decided maybe a lap around the ship might do the trick. He slipped on his black uniform before heading out. The hall was almost as dark as his room. It was easy enough to tiptoe through the officer's wing. He didn't want his squad to tag along this time. They would only provide him with more energy... Maybe not Heike. The habitation deck was silent as he walked out into the main area. Even its unusually bright interior was now dimmed. There were still some soldiers out here, most were on duty and patrolling. The others were like him, trying to get through the night. As he was walking around, he couldn't help but stare out of the only viewport that wasn't on the bridge. The Moskva was still in orbit above Kanto-IV. Carriers, battleships, cruisers, and destroyers all sat idly above the battlefield like stars.

The part of the planet they were deployed to was on the dark side of the planet's rotational cycle. The fighting that occurred there was only a precursor, a taste of what was to come for him and his team. Chaotic battles were the norm for them, being surrounded by enemies with only one escape route made for some crafty ways of fighting. This modern way of urban warfare was entirely foreign to them. Lance didn't feel that all of that sacrifice was necessary for a hundred square kilometers of land. One city wasn't worth five hundred lives and four thousand that would never fight, never be the same person they once were again. Thinking over those events reminded Lance there was one person he needed to visit one last time.

The dimmed corridors closed in on him the closer he reached his destination. It was like the hero's noble mount being swallowed by the basilisk, the serpent king. Lance never quite understood why it was these moments that were the hardest to come to terms with. Battles were easy. Fighting was easy. War was easy. You survived, you killed so it's not you. You killed so it wasn't a fellow operator. You killed so it wasn't innocent lives getting crushed under combat boots. The moment you failed to protect something; is the moment it haunts you for the rest of your life. There was no going back, no do-overs. Only the guilt of not being able to do more.

Lance walked under the sign of the medical wing. He ducked through a doorway before the walls could finish him off. This room was a good room. No one was around, save Oliviana. She was sound asleep, exhausted from the medicine that was pumped into her to slow the progression of her illness. He spent some time in here to watch over her. It wasn't a substitute for not being around when Oliviana wanted to visit with him, maybe this would be enough for now. It was time to make that final visit. Lance got permission to enter the morgue. A bunch of metal caskets lined the walls. Each held the frozen remains of a soldier or another. There was only one that he was looking for. It took some time, but he eventually found it. Lance was taken by surprise to see his name displayed across the info readout instead of his identification number. *Lek Diskul.*

He leaned against the metal box. For a long time, Lance stayed in that position. The longer he stayed like that, the more useless it felt. His voice refused to utter a cry, nor did his eyes shed a tear. This was the part that he dreaded the most. In his mind, Lance knew he was saddened at the untimely demise of his friend, but his heart had to response. Almost as if it was wrung dry and left to helplessly flap in the wind. Maybe he wasn't sad. Had he gotten so used to this that this was his reaction now? Could Lance even consider himself human anymore?

"Captain? Are you alright?" A technician asked waving a hand in front of Lance's face. He must have been so lost in thought that he didn't notice the individual.

"I was just thinking was all." Lance spoke softly.

"Okay. We do provide free counseling services if you need them. I'd take advantage of them if I were you." The technician went off to continue whatever it was he was doing before.

"Right… I'll keep that in mind." Lance replied with uncertainty. The guy must have not realized that Lance was an operator. Before going, Lance took one more hard, long look at the coffin, then went on his way feeling a little emptier than earlier.

A new cycle must have been starting as the lighting grew slightly brighter. Another night had come and gone without him being able to rest. He wasn't surprised in the slightest, just another typical night for Lance. Somehow Lance found himself back in the common area of the habitation deck. That was when he noticed Commander Kurepina and her friend Auri sitting out front of the ship's café. From here Lance could tell that she also didn't get any rest after returning from the surface. That didn't seem to stop the Commander, the two were laughing about something. It was good that she was able to do that with someone and get her mind off of the death that surrounded them. Lance was about to go over and for a quick greeting when someone grabbed the sleeve of his uniform.

"Not so fast Mister Revenant." Rose pulled him in a different direction. She was in a completely different get-up than her normal uniform and it reminded him of the PONI woman that he had worked with. Eventually, Rose found an empty room and closed the door behind them. She studied Lance up and down. "What gives? You look like hell."

"I can say the same thing about you, but that is more or less normal." Lance shot back.

"Again, with this? I've had this problem from before I ever became an operator. And how many times to I have to say not to disrespect superiors?" Rose growled. She reached into her coat pocket and pulled out an envelope. Lance took it when she handed it over to him.

"What's this?" Lance eyed the blank envelope and checked to other side for any clue as to what it was for.

"I found it on my desk with a note saying that only you can lay eyes on the inside. Right now, only you and I know about this secret envelope." Rose answered.

"I assume it's a mission meant only for me then. Should I let the commander know?" Lance asked. He noticed that the seal was already broken on it.

"It would be best not to, the seal on the top of the page is from PONI." Rose warned.

"You did read it, didn't you." Lance commented.

"How is that all you got! For your information, I didn't read it, I just peaked at the contents." Lance wanted to point out the flaw in that logic but decided not to.

"If you can get in trouble reading this then why?" Rose looked at Lance like he was dumb.

"Listen here, you may be disrespectful to me, but you're one of *my* operators, my subordinate. Yeah, Kurepina is the overall commander, but I had you first. What I'm trying to say is that I'll always take care of my team and look out for their best interests. If there is something that I think you guys can't handle, then I'll simply refuse to accept that order."

"How often has that ever happened?" Lance let a grin slip.

"Well, you're just too good at what you do. I'm grateful that I have someone to rely on for these types of missions." Rose proclaimed proudly. She opened the door and looked over her shoulder. "Be careful out there, Revenant."

Once Rose left the room, Lance took the orders out of the envelope. As she said, the PONI insignia was stamped right on top. He read through it with a grimace. How did Rose think he would be able to do this? When it came down to taking out Vekros, he was more than ready. This target was something that had never crossed his mind. Why would he want to take out another human? Sure, Lance wasn't fond of the regs, civilians, and people in general. That didn't mean he wanted them to die. Why was he tasked with this? Lance had no clue on how to approach this mission. Fighting the Vekros was simple, just destroy them all. On here, the orders did say to leave no witnesses, but what did that constitute as? PONI sure left him with a lot to fill in. The only way for Lance to approach this was to treat the target as a Vekros, as much as he hated the idea. If that one operative from before was here, how would she handle this?

There wasn't a chance of backing out of this one. It was signed by the Chief himself, which could be just for show. How could question orders when he didn't know how they came down or where they came from? There was no use to questioning when he didn't have a say in the first place. He was just a weapon after all to be used however seen fit. Lance went to go see Commander Kurepina, but she had already gone. He wanted to check in with her, considering she got herself into doing way too much work. It was something for him to look forward to after this mission. His team would be fine, so all there was now was to prepare... and avoid the person looking for him at this moment. He had to prepare for the one thousandth.

Evie was starting to get frustrated. She had planned on getting up early and catching Lance as he walked out of his door. Then they would go train in close-quarters combat, one-on-one. Her personal time with him. Yet Lance was nowhere to be found! It was like he had vanished into thin air. It had been so long since the last time they were able to do that together. Now it was all joint training this or specialization training. Man, she sure wished it went back to the simpler days. Was the way they were treated really that bad? It wasn't like they cared much to begin with. So why did things have to change? She was getting tired of following all the breadcrumb trail. Lance had been literally all over the ship. With the few people that were up, it was a surprise that he went by so many. Each time she asked, they pointed her to his last known heading. It wasn't a surprise that he was busy, but this felt a little excessive.

There was no helping it. Evie might as well go back and see if anyone else is up. Maybe the next time she saw Lance, they could do that training. This was the bad part being in between missions. Unless you were boots on the ground, things tended to go by slowly. *Seriously, things were better when it was just us. At least I wasn't bored out of my mind!*

Evie leaned against a guardrail. It's not like today was a total loss. She could go to the gym with Ryder and A'Darrion. There was that arcade thing she had yet to try. Perhaps the movie theater, they had an extremely rare movie being shown. Resting wouldn't hurt either. A tap on her shoulder had her ready to mouth off whoever thought they could bother her only to be face to face with the commander and her friend.

"Commander?!" Evie wasn't expecting her, or her friend with that untrusting glare.

"Sorry. You looked like you had a lot on your mind." Kurepina apologized.

"Uh- No need! I was only thinking about what to do now that I have all this time off." Evie replied.

"You can join us then. I'm sure Auri could use some company. Right?" Kurepina looked over her shoulder at her friend.

"You're the commander." Auri didn't sound like she liked the idea.

"Please don't be like that Auri." The commander pleaded.

"I just remembered; I have to call my parents. We'll catch up later." Auri scurried off. Commander Kurepina stared off at her friend. Evie stood there awkwardly, not sure what or why there was tension between those two.

"If I'm causing any trou- "

"Do not finish that!" Kurepina interrupted. "We haven't talked much, so I think this would be a good time to get to know one of my soldiers better."

"If you say so." Evie didn't understand what there was to know. She had no interest in the commander... Maybe one or two questions. "So, what were you doing before seeing me?"

"Nothing special. I was just catching up with Auri, but you see how things are." The commander's thought trailed off.

A couple minutes awkwardly passed by. What was Evie even doing? Since when did she shy away from a conversation? Why was she talking to her anyway? She was supposed to not like the commander, not exactly anyway.

"Ugh! Come with me." Evie grabbed the other girl's wrist.

"Where?"

"Just be patient." Evie didn't hide the irritation.

There really was only one place they could go. The way things were now, Evie could not carry on a conversation with this little princess. She didn't even know how to speak to the commander. Her next best option was to add more people. At least two more girls came to mind. Luck was on Evie's side, the two girls she was looking for were where they were supposed to be, plus more. Chika, Heike, Fio, Rose, and Spiritwalker were all together. From the sound of it, they were brainstorming tactical formations. That's the way Evie heard it.

"It's nice to see you Evie, dear. Oh! Looks like a special guest is in tow." Chika noticed the two new people. The other girls all said their greetings.

"What brings you guys here?" Spiritwalker asked.

"We both got stood up." Evie replied quickly.

"I certainly did not!" Kurepina defended.

"Aww, did Lance do that to you commander?" Chika pitied.

"Oh- No, I haven't gotten the chance to see him." Kurepina shifted on her feet. "You can call me Lera- But whatever make you guys comfortable!"

"Haha! Sounds good to me, Lera!" Chika wrapped an arm around the commander, which made the receiver happy. Now Evie felt bad. She was the one who wanted to see Lance, but now the commander was getting the attention. It was her fault for bringing Kurepina here in the first place, so it was deserved.

"I see you have your headphones down, Heike." The commander noticed.

"Yeah. I haven't felt the need to listen to his as much recently." Heike replied absentmindedly.

"Glad to hear it." Kurepina said happily.

"Commander, I know you've been busy, and work is probably something that you relent currently, but can you help devise more formations. Losing Lek was a blow, but that medic that Lance roped in allows for a multitude of possibilities."

"I don't mind, Rose. It's good to see how accepting you guys are of allowing a reg join the team." Kurepina commented.

"We just follow your example. Keep it up, commander." Rose replied.

"Please, you give me too much credit Rose." Kurepina waved it off like it was nothing. "None of it matters if people don't accept change, so it really is everyone."

"Stop being so humble. It may come off as weak to someone." Chika teased.

"I- don't know what you mean." Evie rolled her eyes at the commander's reaction, which no one saw. She decided to quietly slip away. Her job was done, now it was time to prepare to clean her rifle. Maybe she'd run into Lance on the way.

The shuttle doors opened up to the one bay hanger of the destroyer, EENS Allen M. Sumner. Lance wasn't surprised to see the uniform of an agent from the Planetary Order National Intelligence. His uniform was slightly different from the other agent he worked with before. Without even looking, the agent waved his finger for Lance to come over. With bag in tow, he went towards the red-coated agent. The crew members left simultaneously. It all felt odd, like a certain book he read. In that part, the character was executed on the spot. That wasn't going to happen here, but it was better to keep your guard up against strangers.

"It's nice to see that Revenant is punctual, as a weapon should be." The man stared ahead of him. He had a thick accent that was slow and deliberate that didn't really fit with the words he spoke.

"You followed the instructions. Go straight to your quarters, engine deck, fifth corridor, room six." The blonde-haired agent left him alone. That was some greeting. He thought he would have been used to it, but after staying on the Moskva for nearly a year, it felt strange.

The PONI operative didn't say anything about any more orders. Looks like it was just going to be him for some time. Lance instinctively reached for his mask. He was an outsider on this ship. The mask would hide his face... but why would he want to do that? There wasn't any need to where it just yet. Then why did he want to put it on so much? This wasn't Lance's first time on a destroyer. In fact, he had used this specific destroyer countless times. Finding his way down the corridors was no problem. A low hum from the nearby reactor brought a sense of comfort, though a part of him felt out of place. It was probably just his mind being out of rhythm. The room wasn't much, it was basically a storage closet. As he always did, Lance traced the vertical lines on the left wall. All were marks representing the comrades he lost.

He pulled out his knife and began making more scratches. His time away allowed for three more to be lost to the enemy. One before Verdant Prime, one at Raveset, and Lek. After finishing the scratch marks, he took a step back to look at the dozens upon dozens of fallen soldiers. A massive pain hit Lance's head like a hammer. His vision blurred and he staggered a bit, then it was gone. Lance rested his head against the bulkhead. Everything about this mission was very vague, other than that he was assassinating someone from the Terran Revolutionary Front. The timeframe was still up in the air. It could be a month or just a couple hours at most. All of this thinking wasn't getting him anywhere. He'd just have to wait for orders.

Unlike Lance's predicament earlier, this one bothered him more. He was, after all that work to tire himself, ready to rest. The only thing was that his team and the commander were now far away from him. Not being able to confide in them was strange. It was probably from the habit of being able to call on them if he ever had the need to. Even if he knew that, there was that feeling that told him the exact opposite. Lance thought about it for some time with no answers. His eyes were starting to get heavy. Maybe just the thought of his comrades put him at ease.

It was dark, with only the vague silhouettes of trees that resembled humanoid figures that solemnly stood vigil. The branches dangling like arms over a ledge. The sap running like blood from a fatal wound. The wind howled in pain into his ears.

Those trees then slowly started to morph into people. The branches became their broken limbs, blood ran like a river, and the wounded cried out in misery. Lance covered his ears to keep the voices out, but they emanated from his head. It was all his fault.

Something seized his arms and forced them out. It pulled on his legs so he couldn't hide. His eyelids were forced open to a scene of carnage. Comrades that he had long left behind fell in front of him. Their accusing eyes pierced his soul. Lance wanted to reach out and save them, but his body refused to move. The bodies of the fallen then sank below the mud and blood.

I'm sorry! I'm sorry that I couldn't save you! I'm sorry that I was too weak! If only I had been stronger. If I was better. You wouldn't have left me here. Come back. Iron Hand. Captain Marsh. Vaughan... Caroline...

The black returned. An empty abyss stretched out all around him. Then the light slowly brightened like a sunrise. Things moved too fast for him to see, but Lance caught glimpses of the scene. A ship falling towards the ground. Four sets of metallic chips. A once cheerful voice called out in sorrow.

Lance awoke in the middle of lights out. He didn't know how it was possible, but he ended up sleeping an entire day somehow. Another nightmare had come and gone. That last part was weird. It wasn't something he typically had. The blinding light, vague images, and yet was all familiar to him.

"Good morning, sunshine. Or should I say good night?" Came the slow voice of the PONI operative. Lance shot up faster than a mortar round. The man's lips curled up.

"Come now, Revenant. You got work to do." The agent silently slipped from the doorway. Already, Lance was in a foul mood. Having to sort through his thoughts was enough without the likes of some random agent catching him unawares. Heaving himself up, he picked up his bag and followed after the PONI agent. Just like it had been the day before, there wasn't a single soldier patrolling or on guard. This mission was being kept under wraps. His target wasn't just any target then. They must be someone high or important in society. How much he hated calling another human a target. The agent waited patiently for him at the end of the corridor. When Lance caught up, the agent continued on with Lance trailing. They were heading back to the single ship hangar. He wasn't expecting them to have arrived at their destination this quickly. What missing a day does to your routine.

"Here's what I have for you. When you get to the surface, head right immediately after disembarking the shuttle where you'll meet Agent Frost. More instructions will be available then." The PONI operator motioned his hand at the shuttle.

"You're being too vague with only parts of the orders." Lance commented.

"Not. My. Problem." The agent pronounced each word. He tossed over a bundle at Lance. "That's your target info."

Lance entered the shuttle as he opened up the bundle of files. For the size it was, there wasn't much actual information. The most Lance got from it was the target's name, Mark Trottwine, and his occupation. The target was an Aurelet crystal mining tycoon. He owned a couple dozen mines across the Harpy Cluster. His net worth was enough to buy a couple dwarf planets for himself. Lance was only guessing, not fully understanding how currency works. The shuttle interior lighting began to blink, signaling the descent. Lance continued reading, noticing that there was a pattern to Trottwine's schedule. It was something for him to start formulating a plan. If he wanted, he could just outright take him out, but Lance wanted the least amount of risk possible. Seeing this now made him understand that this mission really could take an extensive amount of time. That wasn't want he wanted. He had to get back to Commander Kurepina and the Moskva as soon as he could.

Doors opened to a steady rain as the ground crew scrambled to finish the landing procedure. Lance went right just as he was told to do. This led away from the main part of the military base and more of a storage area. The so-called Agent Frost was supposed to be around here. Lance had to search for the agent since he wasn't given a precise location. It didn't take him long to find the agent engrossed in his hand-held device. The man had a convenient overhang so the rain wouldn't get anything wet. A large vehicle was left running just around the corner.

"Agent Frost?" Lance called. The agent jumped slightly like he wasn't expecting him. *PONI's greatest operatives, right?*

"Perfect timing. Revenant, I presume." Agent Frost had an annoying, nasally voice.

"I am." Frost glanced down at Lance's hip curiously.

"What's with the mask?" The operative questioned.

"To be used." Lance replied curtly.

"If you say so." Frost nodded. "In the car then."

"I have a question." Lance spoke.

"Ugh. Get on with it, we don't have all day." Frost groaned.

"When it said leave no witnesses; what does that mean?" Lance asked.

"You're the gun, figure it out. What to guns do best?" Frost hinted.

The passenger doors automatically opened when Agent Frost was within ten feet of the vehicle. Lance was surprised to see that there was no driver in the driver's seat. A giant screen displayed their heading as well as other things. It was like a drone, but a car.

"Crazy right. This is an Arletio. Very luxurious SUV if I do say so. The car has self-driving AI and Arletio doesn't export. That means that you can only get these on this planet." Frost began his rant on this Arletio group. Lance was keenly interested in the SUV itself. Everything else about exports and car models just went over his head, so he only paid attention to the features of the car itself. It was a good piece of machinery, which made him wonder why the EEN didn't use this. The vehicle felt leaps and bounds better than the current armored transport.

It was a long drive, and somewhere along the way, Agent Frost ran out of steam. Now he sat there sipping some iced drink while Lance flipped through a book he picked up. The planet that Lance was on only had one military base, a rather small one at that. It would have been faster to get where they needed to be by plane, but Frost was enjoying himself too much in here. The book Lance was reading was unlike anything he had ever read before. He wasn't sure if that was a good thing or a bad thing. The story was good, engaging plot, excellent writing; it had plenty of action and some science stuff that made his head hurt, but it also had something that was semi-foreign to him. It wasn't like he had no experience with it, it was something he wasn't good at, so he stayed away from it. For some reason, Kurepina came to mind.

"Listen up, your name is Davis Rogers, and you live in Skyline Apartments room number thirty. I'm sure you can handle the rest. We'll know when the job is done." Frost gave Lance a sharp look as Lance's door opened. He took his bag and watched the SUV drive away. Looking behind him, the sign that read Skyline was blinking off and on. Obviously faulty wiring. The building was also run-down, like they picked it up from a warzone and dropped it in the middle of a metropolis. He wasn't going to say he was surprised that this was the outcome, but Lance had gotten used to the environment the commander provided. It was almost like the agent was throwing his lifestyle in Lance's face. Sure, Lance may be a weapon created to destroy the threat to humanity, but he would like to see that agent try Lance's role for five seconds.

The set of rooms that the agent called an apartment didn't look as bad as the outside, but that wasn't saying much. It was dark and dingy, yet this was the type of environment he lived in for years. Though, he had heard so much from the commander and a couple other officers of civilian life. Lance had a small taste of it before. At the time, he disliked it, but lately had been quite curious.

Now wasn't the time to explore that. A job needed to be done so he could get back. No time to settle into things, just move the obstacles out of the way now. He no longer had the files. Good thing he memorized every detail that was on the pages. It was time to get to work.

Nearly a week had gone by since Lance had started his mission. Mark Trottwine was one busy individual. Half of the information Lance was given hindered the start of his tracking. Trying to gather new information while staying on schedule proved difficult. Lance thought he was going to miss his target date when a stroke of luck came by. At the expense of one TRF soldier, Lance was able to nab the businessman's schedule for the end of the week. Lance made sure to not leave any evidence behind or witnesses as ordered. Not that any witnesses were around to see anyways. Trottwine had a three-day conference before going home on Sunday. His spouse was going to be out of town, leaving only at home staff and TRF soldiers. They wouldn't be a problem.

The hour was fast approaching for the assassination to commence. Lance had found a handgun and silencer in the wall, the weapon he was to use. He had a half an hour left of waiting. Missions never made Lance nervous, this one was an exception. Killing another human was wrong. The enemy bared down from all sides, yet people had the gall to kill another human life like it didn't matter. What was Lance's comrades, no, that wasn't right. What was the point of all the soldiers who've never returned if humanity was killing itself from the inside?

The only thing was to hope that this was the first and only mission that he had to do this. It wasn't worth his time. It wasn't worth being away from the people he needed to protect. It wasn't worth feeling sick to his stomach. Lance looked out over the horizon where the star used to be. It was time. Lance slipped through the gated yard with little trouble. One TRF soldier stood at the front door. Lance fired once, rushing and guided the body quietly to the ground. The silencer wasn't exactly quiet, but one could confuse it for a knock. He entered into unknown territory. As hard as Lance tried, he could absolutely nothing on Trottwine's home.

Most of the lights were turned off, save for a few workers. Lance tried his utmost best to avoid the workers. He didn't want to drag them in a war between PONI and the TRF. Trottwine must have felt really safe, since there were hardly any soldiers to speak of. The few he had killed were unarmed. At last, he found a room that had a faint, flashing glow. Lance peeked around the corner to see Mark Trottwine watching a man point at graphs on a screen. Lance tiptoed behind the Trottwine and pressed the gun to the back of his head. Trottwine tensed up in response. Lance wasn't going to give him a chance to turn around and pulled the trigger. Trottwine slumped forward, then fell sideways until he was halfway off the couch.

"Dad!" a voice startled Lance. Two smaller figures ran up in the darkness and wrapped around the deceased man.

"Daddy! Wake up! Please daddy!" the higher pitched voice. Lance was about to flee when those words came into his head. *Leave no witnesses.*

Lance clutched his stomach. He wanted to yell in frustration, in despair. How could he have missed such a major detail? Why? Why was this happening! Flipping off the safety, Lance turned slowly. His heart was beating like a drum and his vision was like looking through a filter. The two figures were still trying to shake the man they called dad awake. Noises outside the room got louder and louder. Lance could hardly keep his gun straight as his hand shook uncontrollably. Then he dashed out the door.

I'm sorry…

Chapter 8

Among the Stars

Things had slowed down a bit after a week. Their departure had been delayed until the week after the next due to a comet's proximity to their planned route. They were waiting for the all-clear from Traffic Routing Wing (TRW), a sub-branch of EEN command that tracked celestial objects and charted safe travel paths. The suggestion did come up to go a different way back, which Captain James shot down in favor of recuperation. Lera was thankful for that decision because Lance had been gone for a week. After her impromptu hangout with her operators, Lera went to look for Lance to check in on him. It wasn't until an hour later that Rose told him he had been sent on a mission. Being rather furious, she had to keep her composure as she drilled Rose for not informing her. Rose responded that it was necessary and wasn't remorseful about it because she knew Lance could handle it.

Then the handler had the gall to ask if she didn't believe in Lance's abilities. That really did stop Lera in her tracks.

Obviously, she knew that Lance could handle missions by himself, but she couldn't find an answer for Rose's question. She only managed to stumble over her words before informing the handler that all future missions had to be approved by her first. To be fair, Rose wasn't entirely to blame, Lance was also at fault for not saying anything either. Did Lera have some choice words for him too when he gets back.

The only thing was that Lera was bothered by not being able to answer that question. It didn't just apply to Lance but all if the operators. All she had experienced was success. Then in this most recent campaign she was without the operators for the first time since she'd known them. It was nerve racking for two reasons. The first being that she had no way at the time to contact them to see if they were alright as part of the mission. Two, she was afraid to fail to live up to expectations. At heart, Lera was fighting to end the war with the Vekros. Recently, she felt that she had developed selfish goals. The biggest being trying to keep up the string of victories. That might not seem bad on the surface, except it was at the expense of the operators. It made her realize that she might have taken their talents for granted, and she wanted to do something with Lance to disprove that, and he wasn't here.

As she was walking by the shooting range, the gleam of a handgun caught her eye. Next to it was a full magazine. What was it doing here unattended? Better yet, who left it here in the first place? She picked up the handgun, noting it was the lightweight version of the MPS-4, or the Four-Mini. Lera loaded the magazine and aimed at the target. She fired five shots, all of which hit near center mass. In no way was she an expert marksman, but that was shooting that she could be proud of. It confirmed that she was able to do something to protect Lance, Heike, Misha, and Caitlin as they retreated.

"Wow! I'm still surprised that our illustrious commander is such a good shot." Rene's voice echoed. She wheeled around to Rene leaning on his arms against a low wall to simulate cover.

"Uhh, illustrious seems a bit much. Were you the one that left this here?" Lera waved the gun before setting it down.

"Sure did. Where did you learn to shoot?" Rene started taking apart the gun.

"They taught us in the academy. Then I learned that shooting a bottle cap off a fence post was not a great way to impress my mom." Rene had a huge laugh at Lera's comment.

"Really? You did that?"

"Yeah! I was excited that I could do it, so I wanted to show my parents. They're a little more... traditional. My dad is a little more open to change, but my mom is completely opposed to everything that I like or do." Lera felt the sudden urge to hug her parents. She hadn't seen them in person since she was shipped off on the Moskva. "I have a question. Why is your callsign a red spider lily?"

"Ah. I didn't choose that name, Chika did. It's her favorite flower before everything and we tweaked the name to it. Other than that, she never gave a clear reason as to why she chose it. In turn, I came up with hers and it wasn't anything special. It was the only thing I could come up with at the time, yet she was so happy when I came up with it."

Lera watched Rene's facial features as he reminisced. It was clear to anyone who paid close attention to see how happy he was. It must be hard to try to have a sense of normalcy having the life of an operator. To try and live the same life you once had. Was he one of the kidnapped from Athena? Although, seeing how happy he is, having a relationship like that did sound kind of nice.

"Something on your mind?" Rene asked out of nowhere.

"Huh? Not particularly. I'm just... confused? Some things have happened and I'm just trying to sort it all out." Lera wasn't sure if she was being too vague, not that she wanted anyone to know. Rene had the hint of a smile as he was cleaning the pistol.

"Don't worry Commander, I know what it is. Whoever this person is, go after them, they might feel the same way." Lera tried not to be too obvious, but she definitely knew her face was red with him being so accurate. Rene finished cleaning the gun and putting it back together. He flipped it around and handed it over to her.

"Oh! I already have a sidearm." Lera shook her hands.

"This one is better. Operator issued and served at a certain someone's side well for a long while." Lera took the handgun and tilted her head quizzically.

"Who would that be?" She asked.

"Check the bottom of the grip." Rene suggested. Lera did just that and found the initials *LF. Wait, is this-*

"These are his initials." Lera traced the two letters with her index finger. It made her think harder about Rene's earlier comment. "I'm... not sure how I feel. Is this, uhh- "

"I wouldn't have mentioned anything otherwise. Don't overthink it too much Commander." Rene put up to thumbs at the end of his reply.

"I see why you and Lance work so well together." Lera studied the handgun a little more.

"We make it look easy; it still takes some work." Rene shook his head. "You make it effortless Commander."

"Lera is fine, Rene." Lera voiced.

"Nope. I want someone else to say it before I do." Rene gave her an extra holster for the new weapon.

"Well then... It looks like I have some work to do." Lera smiled. Thanks to this conversation with Rene, she felt rejuvenated. Unlike the troubles of war, this felt freeing. No wonder the other operators said that Rene was like the older brother to them all. He had a way to put people at ease and their worries into something they could handle. Will Lera be able to do it herself? Once the sorted out her mind, only then will that answer be clear.

She and Rene went their separate ways after their conversation. There was progress being made between her and the operators. At one point, all of them would give her strange looks every time she was around. Now, they sought her out when they needed something. It was safe to say that they trusted Lera. Things could only go up from here. Humanity, albeit very slowly, was retaking territory lost in the first half of the war.

Lera managed to change the culture on the Moskva with the help of others. Everyone was willing to pull together in an effort to win this war. The operators have become a huge part of this. She was starting to see that their futures weren't so bleak after all. Lance wasn't going to have to worry anymore. At least she hoped.

A notification came in of a shuttle landing. There wasn't much else for Lera to do, so she headed over to that area of the hanger. The vessel that had landed was not from the Moskva. It had different markings from what the pilots stationed here would paint. Then a familiar animal came up to greet her.

"Ooh, hi Dog." Lera attempted to sidestep away from the dog as he began sniffing around her boots. She tried to go straight for the shuttle, but the dog just kept getting in her way. All she wanted to do was see what was on that ship.

"This is why cats are better!" She hissed at Dog.

"He just wants for you to pet him." A tired voice sounded in front of her. Lance stood with arms crossed, leaning up against a crate.

"Like I'd want to pet that thing." Lera shot. Lance whistled and Dog went and sat behind him. Then he turned to face her. The first thing she noticed was how exhausted he was both physically and mentally. Lance moved like a defeated boxer. Everything was just sluggish.

"Commander. Have you taken care of yourself this past week? You look like you could use the rest." Lance reached out at started to pet Dog.

"I'm not going to answer that. I don't think you can harp on me about that considering you look in worse shape. I apologize for not being able to provide any support."

"There's nothing to apologize for commander. Plus, I'm pretty sure I look like this after every mission. I feel just fine." The slightest of a catch in Lance's throat tipped Lera off.

"That is such a bold-faced lie that even a blind man could see it. What did you do on your mission?" Lance's body stiffened when she asked that question. His eyes darted back and forth for a second.

"I, don't think I'm allowed to say." Lance hesitated.

"It's okay, I'm your commander. I say it's okay for you to tell me." Lera took a step forward. She could see that sweat began to form on his brow.

"I said I don't want to talk about it!" Lance snapped suddenly. Lera instinctively took a half step back. Lance was not known for raising his voice ever, even during high adrenaline situations. Lera didn't know if she should take another step forward to console him or take a step back and give him some space. She was close enough to him that she could attempt an embrace, but she ended up staying put.

"Sorry. I- uh. It was just my one thousandth mission." Lance avoided eye contact with her.

"Okay. You're not in the best of moods because of that?" Lera finally took a step forward and placed a comforting hand on his arm.

"Yeah, let's go with that." Lance replied softly. Lera didn't like seeing Lance like this. He never had a defeated look on his face, as much as he said he doesn't. Thinking of what could raise his spirits, something quickly came to mind.

"Go get cleaned up and rest for a while. I'll come get you later, okay?" Lance had done things to keep her spirits up. It was about time that she returned the favor. There was also the matter of having two new people join the team and doing something to welcome them would be nice.

"Copy that, Commander." Lance replied meekly. Except the hint of relief in his voice made her feel better. *Now, time to go commandeer a kitchen.*

Oskar patiently, but intently listened to Auri prattle on about Lera. This type of thing had increased over the course of the year. Her complaints were all very trivial. Something he himself would never notice. They were stuff that could never bother him. It was only human nature to seek out companionship with others, not just with a small circle of subjects.

"I thought I was her best friend. What can they do that I can't?" Auri blew into the straw of her drink, which created an exceedingly annoying bubbling sound.

"Perhaps you're looking at this from the wrong angle. Lera's line of work is more challenging and engaging than yours. Having a close bond to her subordinates provides a great deal of trust between a commander and the one's receiving orders."

"Are you saying that my position is less important?" Auri insinuated. He came to the conclusion that he had said something wrong.

"Not at all. Your job is indispensable. Without your precise calculations, we could crash into a moon. Not least of all the ability to- "

"Okay, Oskar. Sorry. I'm just frustrated. I thought we did this so we could stick together. Now, it feels like I'm just getting tossed aside, ya know." Auri looked off to the side, cheek resting in her hand as she slowly sipped through the straw. Of course, he didn't understand what she said, but he knew well enough that she felt hurt.

"If something is on your mind, wouldn't it be better to talk to her about it?" Oskar suggested.

"And cause a bigger blow up than last time? No thanks, but I appreciate the gesture." Auri slid the now empty cup to the center of the table. "I have a diagnostics check to perform. Talk to ya later."

Oskar checked his watch. Perfect timing. There was going to be a reactor test in several hours and he was asked to help supervise the process. Anytime a test on the reactor was done someone from R&D was tasked to take part. Preferably, someone with experience with Aurelet Fission Reactors. There weren't many, as ground-based reactors soaked up most of the individuals with that knowledge. That is why only the larger capital ships had these gargantuan power generators. The three classes of course being carriers, battleships, and battlecruisers.

There were preparations that needed to be made before such a test. Among those tasks, there were other matters that needed attending. Such minor things needn't necessarily need completion, but he wanted them done, nonetheless. Oskar was no infectious disease expert by any means. He did dabble in some research. Approximately over a hundred hours' worth.

All of this was done before being stationed on this ship. He quickly forgot about it as he saw no use for it at the time. That was until he met a little girl named Oliviana. She had been stricken by something that defied the known way of germ theory. In fact, it was unknown how or why some people contracted this disease in the first place and not others.

With the help of Dr. Edwards and his assistant, Novanna Hart, there was some progress being made. As for now, it was about the same as many other powerhouse researchers on Earth had concluded, that they couldn't solve this mystery disease. All he had to do today was prepare for a round of observations and tests for the next day. Unlike his medical colleagues, he would solve this conundrum. Until then, he had some rather pressing work to get to. That reactor wasn't going to keep itself stable after all.

Lance sat on his bed hunched over looking at the floor. His hair was still partially wet and dripped onto the ground. The cries of those kids echoed in his ears. He couldn't do what he was supposed to do, leave no witnesses. They were only kids; it was bad enough he had taken almost everything else away from them. Bad? Is that all he could chalk it up to? Lance didn't deserve to come back after what he just did. That familiar feeling from the not-too-distant pass crept up his spine. The darkness that threatened to swallow him whole, its tendrils wrapped around him climbing ever closer. All he could see around him was that darkness. Then a knock at his door. He got to the door and found the Commander waiting. She didn't have her cap on, not that was something he was against.

"Are you ready?"

"Yeah."

"Jeez! Your hair is all wet. Did you even try to dry it?" There were a couple more pointed questions from Kurepina, and he couldn't find more than two words to say. Lance could only half listen to her talk about all of the things that happened while he was away. His mind was preoccupied, no matter how hard he tried to fight it, Lance knew part of his grip on reality had slipped. Things were too distorted, dull, and lifeless. Then a softness slipped into his hand. Lance didn't realize his eyes were closed until this moment, and it suddenly got a lot brighter.

"Come on. Let's get this over with quickly. If I knew you were this tired, I would have planned this another time." Lera led him along by the hand. She opened the door to a conference room for briefing; everyone was there. His team, the handlers, the three recent newcomers to the circle, and now the Commander too.

"There he is! 'Bout time, Captain!" Ryder shouted. Lance didn't know who, but someone had guided him to a chair while the Commander went to the front of the room. Questions came at him left and right, and he answered them the best he could. It felt just like any other normal day. A pot clanging brought the roar of voices to silence.

"Attention! I set this up to recognize your efforts. Thank you for all of your hard work! Also, I want to welcome our two newest members to the fold. Emma and Caitlin, I can't wait to continue working with you! Now I made this as a show of my appreciation, so I hope you like it!" Kurepina opened the pot and began serving what was inside. A plate was brought to him by Rose, a scent he had nearly forgotten entered his nose. It smelled just like the meal he had at that restaurant. Lance picked up the fork, got some of the noodles on it, then brought it to his mouth. It tasted just like the pasta he had with Kurepina. Then he thought back to when she told him that she'd make it for them when they all were back together.

Lance looked up to see everyone having a blast. Rene and Chika sat side by side; Heike, Misha, Olivier, Edward, and Fio all were engrossed in some lighthearted conversation. Ryder, A'Darrion, and Evie were enjoying themselves. Shi, Ivy-Rose, and Noah laughed with Emma and Caitlin. Abigail looked like she was being some sort of annoyance to Commander Kurepina as she snapped at the intelligence officer. Then, just barely, Lance thought he could make out the outline of Lek in the corner; he blinked, and the outline was gone. Lance settled his eyes on Kurepina, smiling as she went from group to group. Whatever was on Lance's mind before was merely background noise now. What he wanted was right in front of him. If only things could stay like this, all of them together. If there was a way, he would stop at nothing to keep it that way. To keep...

His family among the stars.

Epilogue

Raiders

This ship's captain was driving him insane. They were a lot more resilient these days than when he was in the navy. It took a lot of "convincing" to get this captain to do what he wanted. It was a shame that the captain thought the execution of the entire crew was worth the sacrifice. The man surely had a different tune when his family was being threatened next. Guess he should have started with that if he wanted the captain to do what he wanted. The EENS Republic was going to be the perfect set up for what he wanted to do, well, what his boss wanted him to do. Thankfully they thought the same and that's why they made a great team.

"There. The distress signal is set. Please, leave my family out of this. I just want to see them." The captain pleaded. Mads nodded at Cobra. "Wait plea- "

The captain's plea turned into gurgling as Cobra slit the man's throat. *Oh, the sweet sound I've so very missed!* Mads sat in the captain's chair and watched the life drain from the man.

He didn't think it would be this easy to get on an EEN vessel. This would never have happened in his heyday. The current EEN has certainly grown too soft to his liking. That was why he wanted to flip it on its head. To watch the despair of the weak, and the rise of the true kings that would change humanity.

With a flick of his wrist, the Terran Revolutionary Front vacated the ship. Once a little thorn in their side was taken care of, the TRF was poised to strike. It just had to wait for a certain partner to finish their preparations. Mads couldn't wait for that rose to perish. He couldn't wait for that thorn to drown in his own blood. He would never forgive them for ruining his plan. Now wasn't the time for that, but one day- One day, Mads will have the last laugh.

<URGENT:EENSREPUBLIC:..---...:END>

Afterword

What's up everyone? I have to make this pretty brief since I'm almost at the page and word count limit. As you'll see, I prettied things up a bit and it'll read easier. Now to the story... For those that read it, interesting twists, right? Not expecting any of that, maybe? And for those that are reading this first, Lera, Lance and the team continue their fight. I finally got to write our first space battle, this took a lot of thought as I wanted to try and make it more grounded in reality. Although saying this, space combat is still sort of fantastical. Those who haven't read the story, you might want to stop here and go read first.

So, in terms of content for this story... It's a lot, hence why I have so little to write here. Let's just say that things are starting to heat up, connections are being made, and the past isn't easy to forget. Did I mention that this is still only the set-up? That's right! All of this, and I'm only still setting the story. Volume 3, that's when things are really going to take off.

Thank you to all that helped in the creation of this volume. Your insights were invaluable as always! None of this would be possible without you, the reader. I thank you so much for your support and sincerely hope you've enjoyed the read! I really can't stress enough how thankful I am to have your support, and I hope I was able to, even for a moment, transport you to another world. On to the next volume! Charge!

Earth Exploratory Navy

Valeriya Kurepina: Second-in-command of the EENS Moskva and its operators.

Lance Field: Captain of the operators of the EENS Moskva, Revenant.

Rene Carey: Captain of Cerberus Squad, Lycoris.

Chika Nagata: Captain of Hellfire Squad, Dove.

Heike Herreshoff: Captain of Fenrir Squad, Tauchender Adler.

Ryder Griffin: Vice-Captain, Minotaur.

Evie Day: Expert marksman, Killshot.

Lek Diskul: Explosives expert, Shockwave.

Olivier Daucourt: Operator/Pilot, Paladin.

Edward Eovaldsson: Operator/Pilot, Fanged Demon.

Fiorenza Cirino: Operator/Pilot/Painter, Silent Rain.

A'Darrion Joyner: First in the fight, Damascus.

Mikhail Perezhogin: Infiltrator, Specter.

Ivy-Rose Gibson: Handler of Cerberus, Spiritwalker.

Noah Stone: Handler of Fenrir, Stonewall.

Shi Yuhan: Handler of Hellfire, Rose.